SAFARI ENCOUNTER

Very much against her inclination Jenny had had to accept that she couldn't go on running her father's game park alone; that she would have to let the forceful Joshua Adams virtually take over. But Jenny's real problems began when Joshua took over her heart as well!

Books you will enjoy
by ROSEMARY CARTER

FACE IN THE PORTRAIT

Now that, after three years, she had met Jason Peel again, Cindy knew that at all costs she must keep from him the fact that her little boy Jeremy was his son; after all the heartbreak she had been through she didn't want anything to do with Jason, ever. But Jason, she soon found, was not to be got rid of as easily as that . . .

DESERT DREAM

The only way Corey could get herself on to Fraser Mallory's expedition into the Kalahari Desert was to disguise herself as a man—but she really couldn't expect her disguise to remain undetected for long; nor was it. But the subsequent problems that faced her were quite different from the ones she had expected!

KELLY'S MAN

It was Kelly's fiancé's fault, not hers, that George Anderson had been injured—but it was Kelly who was doing her best to make amends, helping George's wife to go on running their hotel in the Drakensberg mountains. How galling, then, after all her efforts, that Nicholas Van Mijden should persist in thinking of her as just a spoiled rich girl!

MAN IN THE SHADOWS

Stacy knew that the mysterious 'Brett', whom she had encountered on a lonely spot on the Natal coast, was in fact her husband Greg, who had lost his memory. Should she tell him who he really was—when it also meant telling him what a disaster their marriage had been from first to last?

SAFARI ENCOUNTER

BY

ROSEMARY CARTER

MILLS & BOON LIMITED
15–16 BROOK'S MEWS
LONDON W1A 1DR

First published 1981
Australian copyright 1981
Philippine copyright 1981
This edition 1981

ISBN 0263 73600 8

Set in Monophoto Plantin 11 on 12 pt.

Made and printed in Great Britain by
Richard Clay (The Chaucer Press) Ltd,
Bungay, Suffolk

CHAPTER ONE

'YOU'LL have to make a decision regarding Impalavlei.'

'You don't mean I should sell it?' Consternation mingled with astonishment in a pair of violet eyes, elfin-like in an oval face that seemed almost too small for it, especially now, when it was drawn and pale with the shock of unexpected grief.

Jenny Malloy was just twenty-three, and yet each time he saw her she looked more like the father she had so recently lost, Daniel Bannister thought. There was the same wide spacing of eyes, the same high forehead, the same suggestion of generosity in the upward curve of the lips.

More particularly, yet more elusive perhaps, there was the same look of the dreamer. In the father this quality had made a man who could live out his life in the near isolation of a private game park in a lonely corner of the bushveld. In the daughter it had made a young woman whose star was slowly rising in the competitive world of Pretoria's interior decorators.

'Selling might be the wisest decision in the circumstances,' the lawyer said dryly. 'There's something you should know, my dear.' He paused just for a moment. 'There's no money in the estate, Jenny. The last three years have been a drain on your father's resources.'

'I can manage.' A smile lit the eyes, bringing sudden colour to the elfin face, so that Daniel Bannister, who had watched Jenny grow up, was struck anew by her loveliness. 'I have my career, Daniel.'

'You've been doing well, Jenny?'

'Pretty well. I'd like to keep on with it when I'm married.'

'You've set the date, then?'

'Not yet, but we will. In fact I'm seeing Bruce tonight.' Violet eyes grew thoughtful as she remembered her fiancé's strange tone on the telephone earlier in the day. 'Tell me about Impalavlei, Daniel.'

'You'll have to make a decision fairly soon, Jenny.' The lawyer picked up a pencil and began to make idle squiggles on a paper in front of him. Jenny thought he wanted to avoid looking at her, and wondered why.

'What are my options?' she asked quietly.

'The first one is theoretical only. You could go on where your father left off. But of course it wouldn't work in practical terms.'

He was right about that, she knew, trying to picture Bruce living at Impalavlei, and failing. The thought that such a life would mean the end of her career came only seconds later.

'The second option,' she prompted.

'A sale.' For a few moments longer the pen moved over the page. When Daniel looked up Jenny saw that his expression was thoughtful. 'That wouldn't be without problems.'

'I don't understand . . .'

Once more Daniel Bannister did not answer immediately. At length he asked, 'What do you know about Impalavlei, Jenny?'

That it's home, the place where I feel happiest, and where I can escape in my thoughts when the decorating business gets too hectic. The place where I know every waterhole visited by the wildlife, the pools where the hippos laze away their days and the leafless trees where vultures perch before descending to their pickings. All these things the lawyer knew too. As her father's good friend he had often been a guest at Impalavlei.

Aloud she said, 'I take it the question is not as simple as it sounds.'

'Did your father ever discuss his finances with you?'

The running of the game park had never been complicated. It was too quiet and a little too staid to be a star tourist attraction, but it had nevertheless had its quota of guests who visited it regularly year after year. There was no reason for Jenny's sudden feelings of apprehension.

'Not often,' she confessed. 'There was no need to. Daniel, there's something you're trying to tell me. Stop the suspense!'

'Are you too young to remember Martin Adams?' he asked.

'I remember him well. He was Dad's partner. Didn't Dad take over his shares when he went to live in America?'

'He did, yes.' The lawyer looked at her. 'Jenny,

I take it that you know your father tried to make contact with Martin again quite recently?'

There was no justification for the quiver that chilled her. 'I didn't know . . '

'Impalavlei hadn't been making a go of things financially in the last years. Without money—quite a lot of money—your father would have been insolvent.'

'I never knew.' The whisper came from blood-drained lips. 'Dad never said . . .'

Daniel Bannister sighed. 'Perhaps he didn't want to worry you. He loved you so much, and you came into your parents' life so late, I guess he wanted to protect you from unpleasantness just as he did when you were a child.'

A small chin lifted just a fraction. 'I could have taken it. Did Dad ask Martin Adams for a loan?'

'Yes. He tried to raise money here first, but the South African banks weren't forthcoming. Impalavlei hasn't been—' he hesitated '—hasn't been a viable business proposition for some time. Finally Tom wrote to Martin.'

Years ago, long before Jenny's birth, Tom Malloy had braved a fire to save Martin Adams' life. Her father had not been one to dwell on the incident or to make much of it, but from Martin Jenny had heard the broad outline of the story. The two men had always been friends, hence their decision to go into partnership together. The rescue had created a loyalty in Martin which went beyond the bonds of mere friendship. Jenny guessed that it was this loyalty which would have prompted a loan when conventional institutions were reluctant.

'And Dad was able to raise money?' It was hardly a question.

'He was. But not from Martin.' Brown eyes held an expression Jenny could not define. She saw thoughtfulness and concern. But there was also an odd compassion which seemed inappropriate. The quiver returned to her slender frame, stronger this time.

'Martin had died just a few weeks before the letter arrived,' Daniel Bannister continued. 'It was his son who wrote back to your father.'

'Joshua?' Jenny breathed.

'So you remember Joshua?'

'Slightly.' There was a vague memory of a wiry boy with dark hair and sparkling eyes and a marked impatience for little girls. She had not given Joshua a thought since he had left the game park with his father to live in America. Until Daniel's mention of him just now she had in fact forgotten his existence. In her mind he was still a mischievous boy; impossible to imagine him as a man. And yet Joshua Adams had been at least nine years older than herself. Which would make him thirty-two.

'Did Joshua help Dad?' she asked.

'He did. With only a few questions asked.'

'The old loyalty is still alive, then,' Jenny observed after a moment.

'It was.' The past tense was not lost on the elfin-faced girl across the desk from the lawyer. Her uneasiness increased. 'Now circumstances have changed. Jenny, I've written to Joshua.'

Jenny expelled a breath she did not know she was holding. 'And he's replied?'

'There's been no time, but you must make a decision regarding Impalavlei. With your father's death there's nobody to look after the place. The wise thing would be to put the game park up for sale—subject to Joshua's consent, of course. Whatever money is left, over and above the loan, would be yours.'

Logic accepted the rightness of Daniel's suggestion. Jenny knew already that she could not run the game park herself, and that the only way to do so from a distance would be through a manager, somebody competent who would need to be well paid. For that there was clearly no money.

And yet the thought of selling Impalavlei swept her with sorrow. Sorrow that came of severing beloved roots—roots which had been a constant feature of her life even when she was far away. Sorrow that came from breaking up a home which had represented the utmost in happiness to a growing child. Sorrow that came from placing the property which had been her father's love and joy into the impersonal hands of a stranger.

For Impalavlei had been more than a privately-owned game park, run by Jenny's father as a means of earning a living. Impalavlei had represented a dream to a man who had once been a game warden. He had loved the animals of the wild, and the veld in which they roamed, with a passion that was almost akin to his love for his wife and daughter, and he had used an unexpected legacy to acquire a game park of his own.

How would Tom Malloy have felt if he had known that his beloved Impalavlei was to become the property of someone else; someone whose value system and sense of priorities might be very different from his own? He would have hated it, Jenny thought. With the thought came another. Her father would have hated it even more if loyalty were to lay an impossible burden upon her. As much as he had loved Impalavlei, he had nevertheless loved Jenny more, particularly after the death of her mother, when they had had only each other. Tom Malloy would not have wished Jenny to feel torn between conflicting loyalties now that she had a career of her own and was soon to be married to a man who had little interest in the life of the outdoors.

Strangely the realisation did nothing to alleviate the sudden sense of depression. Perhaps, she thought, time was required before the wisdom of a decision could soften the rawness of emotion.

'What makes you think Joshua Adams will consent to sell Impalavlei?' she asked.

Daniel Bannister had watched silently while one emotion after another had flitted across a face that was piquantly gentle and too transparent. Jenny would have to acquire a mental toughness, he thought, his heart going out to her. Until she did so she would be bruised by the obstacles and frustrations of the business world in which she moved.

'I can't see why he'd object,' he answered her. 'The money was lent to help out your father. I gather Joshua has done well in the States, but I've no doubt he'll be happy enough to put his money into something else.'

Into a better investment, Jenny thought to herself, and knew that the resentment towards a man she remembered only as a boy was unreasonable.

Aloud she said, 'I'm glad Joshua won't stand in the way.'

'Then you *will* sell?'

Violet eyes clouded. 'Perhaps . . . I don't know. It makes sense, I know I can't run the place myself. And yet . . .' She stopped.

'And yet?' he prompted.

'It breaks my heart to think of selling,' she said simply. 'You're the one person who'd understand why. Daniel, I need time. Dad's death . . .'

A hand reached across the desk and took one of hers in a distinctly unlawyer-like expression of sympathy. 'I know, Jenny—you're shattered by the unexpectedness. But don't take too much time, love. The decision could become more difficult that way.'

The restaurant nestled in the hills which surrounded Pretoria. During the day the view from its windows was one which took in the sprawling expanse of the city. At night the place was dark and quiet, a little sedate in atmosphere. Jenny knew that out of respect for her father's memory Bruce had suggested it in preference to the brighter, more sophisticated spots they usually frequented.

Dad had met Bruce only once. They had driven up to Impalavlei and spent the weekend at the game park. There had been little opportunity for Jenny to talk to her father alone, to ask him if he liked Bruce. The two days had been too filled with activity. Jenny, proud of her home and the animals who roamed there, had kept her fiancé out of doors almost every daylight moment. It was only later, on the way back to Pretoria, that it had come to her that she had not asked her father for his opinion. He had not come out with one of his own accord. Next time, she had thought, on another visit, they would talk.

But there had been no other visits. Tom Malloy had been an ailing man for some years. Wounded once by a charging buffalo, he had sustained an injury which had never quite healed. When infection set in it did so quickly. Jenny reached the hospital in Nelspruit, the little town nearest to Impalavlei, just in time to bid him a loving farewell.

Dad would have liked Bruce, Jenny thought now, as she looked at her fiancé. He would have liked his warmth and sense of fun, his gentleness and the sensitivity that was an integral part of his stock-in-trade as a photographer for some of the glossier furnishing magazines. Dad had been a man who loved to be out of doors. Bruce's photographic career often took him in search of interesting scenery, but apart from that his interests were pursued largely within the confines of walls. Nevertheless, there were also common traits in the two personalities which would have made them compatible.

Tonight her fiancé seemed preoccupied. Recalling the strangeness of his tone when he had phoned her, Jenny wondered why. There was an unusal tightness in the curve of his lips, and more than once, when she had been talking to him, his eyes had shifted from hers. She had suspected that they would discuss a date for their wedding. Bruce understood her increased feelings of aloneness and her need for a closer bond with himself. As far as Jenny was concerned there was no need to wait; her father would not have wished a period of mourning to stand in the way of her happiness.

The wedding had been on her mind when Bruce had fetched her fron her apartment some time earlier. She had been sure they would discuss it. Yet now, sensing a strain which she could not define, Jenny wondered if something had happened to upset him.

'Something's bothering you, darling,' she said gently, yet with the directness that has always been a part of her nature.

The well-shaped head jerked up and a pair of startled eyes met hers. Whatever was the matter, it was worse than she had thought, Jenny knew. Not for the first time that day she felt a tremor of apprehension.

For a long moment brown eyes that were flecked with hazel stared into hers, then moved away once more. Jenny told herself that it was only in her imagination that her fiancé's face seemed even more closed than it had been before.

'Bruce . . .?' she prompted.

She saw him jab a fork into a piece of meat with unaccustomed violence. He lifted the fork, then put it down on the plate once more. His eyes turned to hers again, and now they were stormy, defiant.

'I'm going away for a while.'

'Away?' For no reason at all her throat was suddenly dry. 'Where to?'

'The Cape. Hermanus, actually.'

She swallowed on the dryness. 'An assignment?'

The pause was so fractional that only Jenny, who knew him so well, would have registered it. 'In a way.'

'Super!' she managed with a cheerfulness that was forced. 'You . . . you'll enjoy that.'

'You don't understand.' Now Bruce looked distinctly uneasy. 'I'll be going alone.'

He was thinking of her own career. Of the assignment she herself had so recently begun: the furnishing of a penthouse in one of the new glass and chrome buildings that dominated the Pretoria skyline. It had to be that. Selflessness would go hand in hand with the sensitivity that was such an integral part of Bruce's personality.

'If you're concerned about the penthouse . . .' she began.

'It's not that,' he said roughly.

'Bruce . . . darling . . .' Violet eyes gazed bewildered into a face that seemed all at once to belong to a stranger. 'I'll go with you.'

'I'm off at the end of the week.'

And there would be no time for them to be

married before then. Suddenly Jenny thought she understood. Bruce had not pressed her to sleep with him after an initial attempt at the start of their courtship: he had accepted her principles and been content to wait. And now those very principles would stand in the way of their future.

'I'll come with you.' The decision made, her spirits lightened. 'The penthouse just needs some finishing touches. Darling, we can be married in Hermanus. Now that Dad . . . now that he's no longer here . . . there's no reason to be married in Pretoria.'

There was a long moment of silence. When Bruce spoke again his voice was very low, a little unsteady. 'I wanted to spare you, Jenny, but you're making me spell it out. I'm going without you.'

The blood drained from softly curved cheeks and from lips that had a pert upward tilt. Jenny's legs felt so weak that she thought if she had not been seated she might well have fallen.

'What are you trying to say?' she whispered when she could speak.

'I'm going away alone.' A note of truculence had crept into his tone as he repeated the words.

'Then . . .' It was hard to force the words through the bloodless lips. 'You . . . you're saying our marriage is off?'

This time the brown eyes held her gaze. The storminess was still there, hardness too. As if he expected argument and was ready for it.

'I didn't say quite that,' he said flatly. 'But I need time. Time to be alone for a while, to think. Jenny, honey ...' she heard the suggestion of pleading, 'I think we both need time.'

How blind she had been! Stupid too! The signs had surely been there for some weeks now and she had ignored them. A reluctance to set the wedding date, a lessening too in the ardour of his kisses. This last she had put down to thoughtfulness on Bruce's part, to concern that she might not be in the mood for his lovemaking. In the space of just a few seconds her illusions had been shattered.

'Then we're finished, you and I?' she got out.

'No, Jenny.' Two spots of colour burned in his cheeks. 'It's just that ... perhaps we've rushed things a little. We both need to think, to come to terms ...'

Was this really Bruce talking, this shamefaced man with the evasive eyes and the words that a stranger might use? Had their relationship meant so little to him that now, when it was clearly over, he could not find the courage to put the position to her clearly; that he had to resort to transparent excuses?

Blindly she pulled the ring from the finger of her left hand and stumbled to her feet. 'Here.' She thrust it at him, the lovely ring which had once been her most cherished possession.

She was moving away from the table when his hand caught her wrist. 'Jenny! Jenny, wait!'

'For what?' Blinking away the tears that had gathered behind her lids, she looked at him steadily, defying him to shift his gaze.

'You're making too much of this. It's just a . . .' he stopped, searching for words, 'a separation. A . . . a breathing space.'

For just a moment she felt pity for him. Her affection for Bruce had made her see only his strengths. For the first time she saw that he was guilt-ridden and confused, unable to make a decision and accept the consequences. He wanted her to continue to think well of him even after he had rejected her.

'No, Bruce.' Jenny drew herself up, feeling taller than her five feet and three inches. 'Perhaps we'll get together again, I don't know . . . But for the moment you keep the ring.'

His hand released her wrist loosely and she saw his eyes widen in surprise. His mouth opened, as if he was about to say something. But Jenny did not wait to hear what he said. She walked away from the table, quickly and without looking back. She felt, paradoxically perhaps, as if she had had the upper hand in the interchange.

It was a feeling which lasted through the taxi ride back to the suburb of Sunnyside; through the walk along the shrub-lined path to the building where she lived, and through the ascent in the lift to the seventh floor. It was a feeling which proclaimed pride and independence and an insistence that she needed to rely on nobody but herself for emotional comfort.

It was a feeling that collapsed as she opened the door of the apartment, and was assailed by loneliness. Emptiness. An emptiness that was so intense that it seemed to have a shape and smell of its own. An emptiness that pervaded all her being, so that she slumped into a chair, her limbs so weak and drained that she thought she could not move them if her life had depended on it.

Pride had carried her through the last half-hour, Jenny knew. Pride coupled with a determination not to admit, either to Bruce or to herself, quite how much his rejection had affected her. For rejection it had been, no matter that he had tried to soften the blow. He needed time to be alone, he had said. He might as well have told her straight out that he wanted to end their relationship. She thought now that she would have respected him more if he had.

It was dark in the apartment, for Jenny had not bothered to switch on the lights when she entered. Presently she reached out and pressed the switch of the small lamp on the table beside her. In an instant the room was bathed in a soft muted glow.

The emptiness was still there as Jenny looked around her. It was an emptiness which the sight of the room did not dispel. The possessions she loved were all here. There were the two love-seats upholstered in green and white floral cretonne, and the carpets and the curtains in subtler of green and white, the colours blending in a cool loveliness that made the apartment seem comfortable on even the hottest of Pretoria days. There were the pictures, a collection of African art on which she had spent a few months' salary. And there were the ornaments, each one of which had been chosen with the care of a person who loved beautiful things.

All day long she worked at producing beauty in the homes of other people. Always she considered the tastes and the personalities of her clients, as well as the kinds of lives they led. In her own apartment she had pleased only herself, had created an atmosphere and a setting which complemented the various parts of her own being.

Until today the apartment had been a kind of haven. The one place, apart from Impalavlei, where she had felt completely at home. It made no sense that the events of the last hour could have evoked this awful emptiness. And yet it was a quality which she was unable to push away. For Bruce had been a part of her apartment. He had sat in these chairs, had fingered these ornaments, had paged through books that interested them both. They had sat in the love-seat, close together, and Bruce had kissed her and held her while they dreamed of their future.

She stood up abruptly and went to stand on the balcony. The building was at the corner of a busy intersection. Below her the streets were loud with the noise of traffic, the lights of the cars like weaving threads in the neon-lit night. Normally Jenny enjoyed the vitality of this scene, but tonight she was irritated by the incessant bustle and noise. A young couple were on the sidewalk, their arms tight around each other. The sight brought a new wave of unhappiness. It came to Jenny all at once that she would not rid the apartment of its emptiness while the memories still remained.

She did not know when her thoughts turned to Impalavlei. It was only hours since her meeting with Daniel Bannister, yet the trauma of the parting with Bruce had driven their conversation from her mind. Now, as it came back to her, she was swept with sudden nostalgia for the game park which had been her home for the first eighteen years of her life.

She had no need to close her eyes to the liveliness below her to picture the night-time setting of the game park. She could see the main building where her father had had his office and his living quarters; could see the chair where he would sit after dark, smoking his pipe and reading by the light of a kerosene lamp. She could see the fires at points around the fence, the leaping flames keeping the animals from the confines of the camp enclosure. And beyond the fence, where the bush stretched on all sides, would be the life of the bushveld night. There would be the hunger of the hunters and the alertness of the hunted, for in that untamed wildness only the unwary would be lulled into discounting the dangers that came with the dark.

And yet the drama of the animals would be one that was enacted beneath the surface of a hushed serenity. Wincing as two cars escaped a collision with a raucous screeching of brakes, Jenny knew that no such noises would disturb the peacefulness of the game park. It was no wonder that her father had resisted the lure of the city all his life. For the first time it occurred to her that in his obstinate clinging to a simple life there had been a wisdom she had never fully understood.

Sell Impalavlei, had been Daniel Bannister's advice. This morning the advice had seemed sensible enough, for then she could not see Bruce settling down at the game park. It was an obstacle which no longer existed.

Jenny could not run the game park on her own, the lawyer had said as well, and that advice too had seemed valid. Her life was in Pretoria. The break with Bruce had not changed the facts and exigencies of her career.

And yet, as Jenny leaned thoughtfully against the stone parapet of the balcony, the advice did not seem quite as valid as before. There had been times recently when she had experienced doubts about the course her professional life was taking. They were doubts she had tried to discount. She loved furniture, enjoyed experimenting with fabrics and textures and colours. It did not matter that she had had few new ideas of late, that one setting differed from another only in certain essentials. She had not grown stale, she told herself. If she had reached a point in her career where her thinking seemed to have grown static, this was a phase which her colleagues must also experience.

She would never lose her love for design. But perhaps a change was called for. She had thought that marriage might be the catalyst she needed. Now she began to wonder whether change of a different kind might not be even more innovative, if not to her career then at least to herself as a person.

Daniel Bannister had not believed that she could run the game park herself, and never imagining that she might in fact want to do so, she had not argued with him. For the first time she knew that her old friend had been wrong. She *could* run Impalavlei. She had lived there long enough to remember her father's routine.

The sound of the telephone jarred through her thoughts, and, preoccupied, Jenny went inside.

'Jenny?'

She stiffened. 'Yes, Bruce?'

'About tonight . . .'

'Please, there's nothing more to talk about.'

'But there is.' Again the note of truculence she had detected earlier in the evening. 'This needn't be a final break.'

But it is. The knowledge came to her suddenly, absolutely.

'Jenny!' His voice rose as she remained silent.

'Let's leave it now.' She was surprised at the steadiness of her words.

'No.' As if he sensed that he was now the one rejected, it was Bruce's turn to do the pleading. 'We just need time. I'll write to you, Jenny.'

'Your letters won't reach me here.'

'You're going away?'

'I'm going home.' Her voice lifted. 'Back to Impalavlei.

There was a moment of silence. Jenny could picture the look of stunned disbelief in the well-shaped features. It came to her that Bruce had been bored during his stay at the game park, and she wondered why she had failed to realise this at the time.

'You're crazy,' he said finally.

He was right, she thought, but did not say so. She *was* crazy even to entertain the idea. By morning she would have forgotten about it.

But by next morning the idea had taken firm hold.

CHAPTER TWO

THE lawyer echoed Bruce's reaction in slightly more dignified terms. 'Ill-considered, Jenny,' he said.

'No, Daniel.' A small chin lifted, and Daniel, who recognised a touch of Tom Malloy's stubbornness, regarded her thoughtfully.

'You've given it enough thought?' he asked at last.

'A great deal of thought.' She did not tell him that she had lain awake for many hours, and that as the desolation had vanished ideas had begun to chase through her mind. She saw the furrows which creased her old friend's brow and she smiled. 'Daniel, I've never been more certain of anything in my life.'

'I see.' Briefly the lawyer smiled back at her. Then he said, 'You know Impalavlei as well as I do . . . as your father did. I don't have to tell you what you'll be going to.'

'You *are* trying to put me off!' Jenny interrupted, puzzled. 'And I don't know why. Impalavlei is home, *my* home. I'll be happy there, you know that . . .'

She stopped, something in the face opposite her making her uneasy. After a moment she said, 'You do know that, Daniel.'

He did not answer her directly. The eyes that met hers were steady as he said, 'There's something I haven't told you, Jenny. There was a letter in this morning's mail.'

'Joshua Adams,' Jenny whispered instinctively.

'Joshua Adams,' the lawyer confirmed. 'He's coming to South Africa, Jenny. He wants to see Impalavlei.'

'Not just a casual visit, I take it.' She had caught the soberness in Daniel's tone.

'Joshua is a businessman. And, as I said yesterday, circumstances have changed.'

She held out a hand. 'May I see the letter?'

The gist of it was more or less as she had expected. What caught her was the handwriting. Bold and quick and impatient, it was the writing of a man who was strong and confident and in control of himself. A man who was accustomed to imposing his will on others, who seldom encountered opposition. The hand that held the letter trembled.

'Let me deal with him, Jenny,' said Daniel, as he took back the letter. 'Give me power of attorney so that we can sell if Joshua agrees.'

Slender shoulders drooped just for a moment, then squared. The chin lifted again. 'No.'

'All right, then.' The lawyer's tone was quiet, but there was a look in his eyes which the small pale girl opposite him recognised as admiration. 'You go home armed with the facts.'

They talked a while longer. Daniel Bannister made no further attempt to dissuade Jenny from her plan. But there were things she had to know, figures to peruse, financial aspects to discuss.

She was standing up to go when she heard him ask, 'Has Bruce anything to do with this decision?'

She met eyes that were sympathetic and understanding. Daniel was the one person she could not fob off with a facile answer. In any event he would see through it.

'Last night,' she said slowly, 'perhaps he did. But not this morning.' A sparkle lit eyes that were wide and deep and violet. 'I'm going to Impalavlei because that's where I want to be. Don't worry about me, Daniel.'

'I won't.' This time the lawyer's smile was without reserve. 'I do wish you luck, Jenny love.'

It was the hour before sunset when Jenny arrived at Impalavlei. It was one of the times she loved best. Sitting in the car that had fetched her from the station, she stared out at the lengthening shadows and knew that she had been right to come home. The car approached a herd of impala. The graceful gazelles, with their look of newly-washed freshness, were grazing. Their ears were pointed, their eyes were alert.

'Please, stop,' said Jenny.

'Just impala,' said George, the driver, looking at her enquiringly as he slowed the car.

Jenny knew what he meant. The lovely buck abounded in the game park. Sighting a lion was largely a matter of luck. Elephant and giraffe, big and therefore not so easily overlooked, were nevertheless a thrill. But the impala were everywhere. It was precisely for this reason that she wanted to look at them now. For the impala signified home.

'Just impala,' she agreed. 'George, it's so good to be back.'

White teeth flashed in a broad grin. George, her father's right-hand man, had lived at Impalavlei for as long as Jenny could remember. She knew that he would have been deeply grieved by Tom Malloy's death. Knew too that he would have wondered how his own life would be affected by it. If the game park had been sold, a new owner might not have wanted to keep him on. For George was old now; he was no longer the nimble tracker he had been when Tom Malloy had engaged him twenty-five years earlier. George would be relieved that Jenny had returned to take over the running of Impalavlei. His expression, when he had come to her on the lonely platform and taken her bags from her hands, had revealed the measure of his relief.

They went on driving, and every twist and turn of the sandy road was as Jenny remembered it. There was the bridge that spanned the corroded bed of a dry river, and the clump of ghost-like trees just beyond it; gaunt-shaped trees with leafless white-coloured branches. Farther on lay a tract of cacti, tiny red flowers bursting from the tips of their succulent stems.

George slowed the car once to let Jenny watch a giraffe nibble at the leaves of a tall mopani tree; and then again to observe a warthog as it waddled comically over the road. The little animal was quickly lost to sight, camouflaged by the bush and the dust stirred up by the car.

They were near the camp when Jenny turned to the man who knew Impalavlei better than anyone else. 'There's so little game.' Her eyes were troubled.

The gaze that met hers was equally sombre. 'Been a bad year, Miss Jenny.'

'No rain, George?'

'Very little.'

Drought. The scourge of Africa, of the animals who depended on water for their existence. Jenny could remember times when her father had been very concerned. She thought of the corroded river-bed that had been dry for many years now. But moments ago they had passed a vlei. Last year there had been water in the pondlike depression. This year there was nothing.

But if drought brought concern, it was also a factor which Tom Malloy had learned long ago to accept. There were years when rain was plentiful, and when game abounded in the vast tracts of Impalavlei; other years when the streams and pans and vleis were almost dry. At those times the animals wandered away, to the Kruger National Park perhaps, or to one of the neighbouring private game parks, where water might be found.

Tom Malloy's concern during the dry periods had been tempered with the acceptance of a philosopher. He understood the fluctuations of nature and did not rebel against them. If there was a year where rain was scarce, he knew too that the following year could be different. Rain would fall again and the drinking-holes would be full, and the animals would return in great numbers. It was a philosophy which Jenny had absorbed from her father.

The drought was forgotten as the car rounded a bend and the camp came into sight. Jenny had always thought her father had chosen the prettiest spot in the park to build his home. Built high on the slopes of a hill, with a river just below it, the camp had an unparalleled view across a vista of veld. Many was the time that visitors had stood at the fence, binoculars held to their eyes, scouring the bush for game. Often the animals had come to this very spot to drink; the impala and the antelope, dainty-stepping and gracious; baboons, gambolling and comic, uttering loud barks as they crashed through the trees; and most impressive of all, a herd of elephants, plunging their trunks into the water and swishing it over their dusty hulks.

The camp had not changed, Jenny thought, as George drove through the stone gates. At least not outwardly. A scarlet bougainvillaea cascaded over the whitewashed walls of the rondavels, and golden shower and hibiscus made a vivid show of orange and gold in the garden. The rondavels clustered in a semi-circle around the main building, and on the stone steps of an outbuilding stood a row of kerosene lamps ready for the night.

The sight that greeted Jenny was the same as it has always been, peaceful, rustic, serene. Home. Just one essential was gone—the one that mattered. For always before a tall figure had emerged at the first sound of the car. In recent years Tom Malloy had grown increasingly frail, but his welcoming smile had never wavered.

A lump formed in Jenny's throat. She blinked away the sudden tears, for George was stopping the car and the staff would greet her, and they would be distressed at the sight of her grief.

As she opened the door of the car she made a silent promise. Impalavlei will be safe in my hands, Dad. And for no reason at all she thought of Joshua Adams, of a letter written in terse businesslike terms, of a handwriting that bespoke determination and impatience.

The air was still very hot, and would remain so until sundown. Yet for a moment Jenny felt cold. And then, as the first of the camp staff came forward to greet her, she shook herself sharply. The emotion of the last weeks—the death of her father, the reaction of her fiancé—had taken more out of her than she had realised. There could be no other reason why a mere letter should upset her. Forcing a smile to her lips, she stepped quickly forward and said her hellos.

Jenny settled quickly into the life of Impalavlei. The staff, most of whom had worked at the game park for many years, accepted her instructions cheerfully. Not that many instructions had to be given. A daily routine had been established over the years. It worked satisfactorily enough, there was no reason to change it.

She found that her days were fully occupied.

Her father had attended to the administrative duties of the game park himself. Once he had employed a woman to look after the office work, but as the finances of Impalavlei had deteriorated he had taken over these duties also—the correspondence, the book-keeping, the ordering of supplies. All this Jenny did now.

At the present there were three guests at the park. The Andersons were an elderly couple from Pretoria who came now and then to escape the bustle of city life; the third person was an old friend of Tom Malloy's, an eccentric who could happily spend hours at a waterhole with binoculars and a book without ever growing tired or bored. Of the eight guest rondavels six were unoccupied. Checking future reservations, Jenny noticed that they were regular if fairly sparse. Most of the names were known to her; they belonged to people who had been coming to Impalavlei for years.

At the end of the day sometimes, when she stood at the fence and stared out at the darkening veld, Jenny would think to herself how much her life had changed in just a few weeks. Pretoria and her career seemed to have existed in another world. All that was left of that life were the possessions she had brought back with her to Impalavlei. Some of the furniture she had sold, but not all. There were pieces she had grown very fond of. She could not bring herself to part with her curtains and cushions, her pictures and books and ornaments. All the things that had once made the apartment in Sunnyside her own special place, were now in her room at the camp. They made a sophisticated oasis in the rustic simplicity of the game park.

Apart from a postcard, Jenny had not heard from Bruce since their last telephone conversation. She tried not to think of him, for his rejection still hurt. Yet she was beginning to realise that the hurt was more a matter of wounded pride than of loss. Perhaps, as Bruce had said, with time and separation their relationship would be as good as it had been before. Part of her wanted to believe it. Another part told her that if Bruce needed time to be alone, it was what she needed also, and when it was over the conclusions each would come to might well be very different.

She was pruning a wild fig-tree one morning, about three weeks after her arrival at Impalavlei, when a housemaid came to call her; a stranger was waiting in the reception office.

As she put down her gardening gloves, Jenny tried to think who the person could be. She wondered if she had overlooked an expected arrival. Only yesterday she had checked the reservations. If there was one for today she had obviously missed it.

Running a hand through wind-tumbled hair, she made directly for the office. In the doorway she stood still. A man was at the window, looking out. He was tall, broad-shouldered and with a bearing that was strong and athletic. Dark hair curled into the nape of his neck just above the collar of his well-cut jacket. His hands were in the pockets of his trousers, his legs firmly braced and just a little apart. Jenny not have said why his stance suggested impatience, nor could she have explained the sudden quiver inside her.

Quite suddenly he turned, and the quiver increased as Jenny found herself looking into the most compellingly attractive face she had ever seen. His face was long and lean and well-shaped, reinforcing the impression of strength. His eyes, beneath winging brows, were alert and intelligent with laughter lines at the corners. Yet the expression in the grey eyes was anything but amused. If anything, Jenny registered displeasure.

He was certainly not one of the regulars, she knew, feeling suddenly flustered. She moved towards the reservation book that lay open on the counter. If she knew his name she might not feel at quite such a disadvantage.

'Good afternoon,' she said slowly, giving herself time to find his name.

'Joshua Adams,' he said crisply, and with a certain biting amusement, as if he sensed her embarrassment. 'Hello, Jenny Malloy.'

'Joshua!' She stared at him open-mouthed, her body rigid. Later, when she could think, she would wonder how she could have been so foolish as not to have guessed his identity immediately.

Recovering herself, she said the first words that came into her mind. 'You look as impatient as ever.'

A glimmer of amusement lit the dark eyes. 'And you're almost as untidy as I remember you.' And then, his gaze moving over her body—clad in jeans and a T-shirt that hugged firm rounded breasts and a small waist—he added, 'Though in other ways you've changed.'

As warmth flooded her cheeks, Jenny straightened to her full five feet and three inches—a height which nevertheless seemed absurdly small in comparison with the rugged six-footer so close to her. 'Daniel Bannister said you were coming.'

'Ah.' There was an enigmatic gleam in the grey eyes. 'So you were in fact expecting me.'

Jenny was not certain why she was discomfited by his expression, nor why she had the feeling that she was somehow being put in the wrong.

Coolly she said, 'Of course. I saw your letter.' And then, 'If you'd have let me know the date of your arrival you would have been met at the station.'

The expression in his eyes deepened. 'I did communicate with you.'

She stared at him. 'I haven't had a letter . . .'

'When was the last time your mail-box was cleared?' There was no mistaking the contempt in his tone.

'The mail-box?' With an effort Jenny jerked her thoughts to the spot some miles distant where letters were deposited. George was supposed to drive there each morning, but in practice it did not work that way. There was not sufficient mail to warrant his making the trip every day.

Defensively she said, 'It was cleared two days ago.'

'So recently?' he asked very politely.

'Had I known there was something urgent I'd have been to look myself.'

One elegant eyebrow lifted. The gesture was mocking in the extreme. Irritated, Jenny snapped, 'Impalavlei is not an efficiency machine!'

'And that,' he said, his gaze deliberately sweeping the office, 'is something I'm prepared to believe.'

Jenny followed his gaze. The park office had not changed with the years. It was so familiar, so much 'the same', that it was a long while since Jenny had consciously taken in any of its details. As she followed the direction of the alert grey eyes, she found herself looking at the office as if for the first time. She saw the shabby furniture and the worn carpet; the rack where the postcards were kept, the pictures looking somehow faded and unimaginative; the prints on the wall, just a little askew; on the counter the vase of dried proteas, once a lovely arrangement but dusty now and a little bedraggled. On the wall facing the entrance was an impala's head; its horns were cracked and the animal had a woebegone appearance. Like the proteas and the furniture and the postcards, it had evidently been due for replacement some time ago.

Strange that she had needed Joshua's dispassionate gaze to awaken her own conscious appraisal, Jenny marvelled, for she was accustomed to surveying any new room with the eyes of decorator. Yet perhaps it was true that familiarity dulled the faculty of critical perception, so that until this moment she had been unaware of the fact that the office was in need of renovation. A fact which need not be acknowledged, at least not to Joshua Adams.

She decided to ignore his remark. 'You'll be staying a few days?' she asked.

His lips lifted at the corners. Malice? Or merely a disconcerting amusement? 'Longer than a few days.'

How much longer? Jenny was on the brink of asking the question, but did not. Looking up into the strong attractive face, she felt a rush of dismay coupled with an emotion which she could not name. Curling her fingers into her palms, she cleared her face of any expression. 'Then you'll be wanting a room,' she said quietly.

'If you have a spare one.' His manner was polite, in no way suggesting that he knew of the six empty rondavels. Yet Jenny was certain that he did know.

Moving towards the door, she said, still with the coolness that was so alien to her nature, 'I'll see about organising something.'

Without waiting for his reply she moved swiftly out of the office. She knew exactly which rondavel she would give him. The bed was made up and the room was tidy. She could have shown him the way herself, now, without making him wait. It was what she would have done with any other guest. Impalavlei prided itself on its informality, and Jenny herself seldom stood on ceremony.

But something had made her reluctant to take Joshua to the rondavel he would occupy. She quivered at the prospect of walking beside the tall lean man with the broad shoulders, and the eyes that were grey and alert and far too perceptive. She would call one of the maids; Anna would be happy to do the chore in her stead.

When she had instructed the smiling housemaid to show the man in the office to his room, and to bring him sandwiches and tea, Jenny looked down at her hands. She was still holding her gardening gloves. But though she had nothing pressing to do for the next hour or two, her enthusiasm for pruning had vanished.

She walked instead to her room in the main building. The encounter with Joshua Adams had left her feeling strangely restless. Gardening was the very occupation she needed, she tried to tell herself; it would steady her nerves. But she knew too that she wanted to be alone, in the privacy of her room, where there was no risk of seeing Joshua. She needed time before she met him again.

Normally the sight of her lovely room gave her a feeling of joy. Now she did not notice the prized possessions she had brought with her all the way from Pretoria. She only had eyes for the mirror.

She was even more dishevelled than she had realised. Dark hair clung to her head in a damp tangle, and her brow was mud-streaked where her hand had wiped across it. Her cheeks were glowing with an unaccustomed rosiness which spots of dust failed to hide. Even her eyes lacked their usual serenity. They stared back at her from the polished glass in its antique frame, long-lashed and violet, and there was a look in them she had not noticed before, one that she could not quite define.

Sitting down at the dressing-table, Jenny stared at herself for a long time. She was as untidy as he remembered her, Joshua had said, not mincing his words. She struck the table-top with an angry hand. It should not matter that after all this time he had seen her this way. That the impression he had formed at their first meeting might be the one he would carry with him always. Yet oddly it did matter. It mattered more than she wanted to admit to herself.

For Joshua Adams had changed. The wiry boy she had known so long ago had become a man she would not have recognised; a man who was compelling in his impact. Jenny had not needed much time in his presence to know that he radiated an aura of strength and power and arrogant self-sufficiency. Coupled with these qualities were attributes of a more physical nature—an aura of sensuousness and virility, a basic maleness which he seemed to wear as naturally as he wore his extremely well-cut clothes.

In every way possible, he was different from Bruce. He was a type she did not care for, Jenny told herself. Her fiancé was no less masculine than Joshua, but the impression he gave out was of refined gentleness. The maleness she had encountered minutes ago in the office was too obvious to appeal to her.

Quite involuntarily, she found herself wondering how it would feel to be kissed by Joshua. A moment later, appalled, she thrust the thought from her. Joshua Adams had come to Impalavlei on business. Already his contempt for the place where he had once lived was clear. He intended to stay longer than a few days, he had said. Long enough to investigate the finances, was what he obviously meant. She would help him with whatever he wanted to know, for the sooner he left here the better. Better for Impalavlei, where he might be a disruptive influence. Better also, Jenny sensed, for her own peace of mind.

Abruptly she stood up, went to the bathroom and showered, then changed into a skirt and blouse. The skirt, a soft flowing blue, was a departure from her usual jeans. The blouse, demurely round-necked, was yet tight enough to reveal the feminine curves of her figure.

She was crazy, Jenny told herself angrily. In a moment she would change back into the clothes she had worn earlier in the day. There was no reason to make an effort with her appearance just because Joshua Adams had arrived at Impalavlei.

But she did not change back into her jeans. She sat down at her dressing-table and began to brush her hair with swift strokes, savage strokes, as if the very savageness could in some way eliminate the inexplicable angriness from her system.

At a knock at the door she called, 'Come in,' without interrupting the movement of the brush. The caller would be a member of the staff coming to ask something.

The hand that held the brush stopped in mid-air as a lean hard face appeared in the mirror. The breath jerked in Jenny's lungs. And then a moment later, when she could breathe again, she turned, very slowly, giving herself time to summon control.

'What are you doing in my room?' she asked in what she hoped was her most biting tone—and hoped he did not hear her unsteadiness.

The look of amusement was becoming familiar. 'I knocked.'

'I thought . . .' She stopped. She could tell him that she had expected one of the maids, and in return she would get a rejoinder which she could not hope to match. 'What do you want?' she asked instead.

Joshua did not answer. She saw that his gaze was sweeping the room, and knew that he missed nothing. For a few seconds his eyes rested on an ivory bird which was one of her most cherished possessions—a piece with fluid lines and a graceful shape. She could see his eyes in the mirror, and the approving gleam that lit them. She felt an absurd joy, then remembered, almost immediately, that Bruce had never liked the bird. Her fiancé had been annoyed at the money she had paid for it—irrationally annoyed, Jenny had thought at the time.

Forgetting for a moment the animosity Joshua had stirred in her, she was about to ask him if he liked the bird, when she saw his gaze move to herself. The gleam was still in his eyes as they held hers, not approving now, purely mocking. Jenny stiffened as the words froze in her throat. She sat very still beneath a scrutiny that took in her change of clothes, the improvement in her appearance. Joshua knew her annoyance at being surprised looking less than her best at their first meeting, knew too that she was now doing all she could to correct the impression. He made no attempt to conceal that knowledge, for his scrutiny was blatant. Jenny's moment of joy was gone and her cheeks were more flushed than before.

'What do you want?' she demanded again.

As if he did not hear the question, Joshua said, 'Quite a paradox.'

'I don't know what you mean,' she said stiffly, after a moment.

'Sure you do.' His eyes swept the room once more, briefly, before returning to her face. 'You must know that this room is in direct contrast with the rest of this neglected place.' Unexpectedly he grinned, his teeth white and wicked against the gaunt planes of his face. 'And don't bat those violet eyes of yours. You're no innocent little miss, Jenny Malloy. You couldn't have furnished this room if you were.'

'I'm an interior decorator. Does that explain things?' Her voice was bland as she tried to conceal the new emotions he had aroused in her. There was further anger at his patronising attitude towards Impalavlei. There was also a fresh surge of joy at the fact that he had recognised her taste in furnishings and been impressed by it. It came to her, very briefly, that Bruce had never had the power to affect her quite like this.

She said tartly, 'I ask you again—what do you want, Joshua?'

'First and foremost, a tour of Impalavlei.'

'Of course.' She threw him what she hoped was a cool smile. 'We can set out tomorrow after breakfast.'

'We'll go now,' said Joshua.

Jenny stared at him, seeing the firmness of a long jaw, the impression of power in high chiselled cheekbones, the control in dark eyes beneath thick winging brows. He was altogether too sure of himself, she thought. There was no reason why they could not go driving today. Her duties were over for the moment, she would not be missed. Yet it was important that she refuse him. If she did not assert herself now, it might become more difficult to do so later on.

She tried to quell the feeling of excitement that came with the thought of spending time alone with Joshua Adams. He would be a man who would set the emotions of most women whirling. She would make quite sure she was not one of them.

'We'll go tomorrow,' she got out, bumpily.

She braced herself for a verbal rejoinder. It did not come. She was unprepared for the hand that shot out instead, gripping her wrist and drawing it upwards with a languidness that was deceptive. She found herself being pulled from her stool till she stood within a half inch of a long wall of male body. He was so close to her that even without actual contact she could feel the warmth of him through his clothes and hers. She could hear the beat of his heart, could sense the tautness of his thighs. How dared he! she thought, enraged. Just minutes ago she had wondered how it would feel to be kissed by him. Any moment now she would know.

But he did not kiss her. Instead he said, 'Don't fight with me, Jenny Malloy.' His clean breath fanned her brow.

Strength returned to limbs that had been momentarily weakened. Balling her fists, she thrust them against his chest and pushed herself away from him.

'You were always mean to girls!' she threw at him.

He chuckled, as if he knew exactly the effect his behaviour was having on her. The sound of it so near to her was infinitely unnerving. 'Let's get going,' he said.

CHAPTER THREE

THEY had been in the car more than an hour. Jenny drove, while Joshua sat beside her, his face turned to the window. His body was long and loose-limbed in the seat of the Land Rover. To a casual stranger he might appear relaxed. And yet Jenny, though she was hardly more than a stranger herself, felt that he was not relaxed at all. She thought he took in every animal, every tree, the very blades of grass that bent with the breeze.

So far, no more than a few words had passed between them. He had forgotten her too, that was clear. She was the person who drove the car, who made it possible for him to give his undivided attention to the passing landscape—no more than that. It was absurd, Jenny thought, that this fact could give her even the slightest pain.

It was clear also that he had forgotten the incident in her bedroom just a short while ago. Or if he had not exactly forgotten it, he did not think of it either. The physical closeness which had lasted no more than seconds had not touched him at all. Jenny wished she could have said as much for herself.

In terms of time she had spent no more than seconds in his arms. She had not reached the age of twenty-three without spending far longer in a man's embrace. There had been boy-friends before Bruce, and while she had always set certain limits, there had been kisses which she had enjoyed. She had enjoyed Bruce's lovemaking, had looked forward to the time when they would be man and wife and there would be no holding back. There had been occasions when Bruce had tried to persuade her to sleep with him. One evening in particular stood out in her memory.

They had gone dancing, and she had had a little more wine than she was accustomed to, and later in her apartment, when he had pulled her to him, she had been melting and pliant, taking pleasure in the arms that held her tight, in the path of his lips over her face and throat. And then his kisses had become more ardent. He had pushed her back on to the studio couch and she had felt his fingers at the zip of her dress. She had pushed him away. They would wait until they were married, she had said—not for the first time. She had hoped Bruce would see reason, that he would hold her against him again in the lovely warmth they had shared until that moment, but instead he had stiffened and stood up and said an abrupt goodnight. Jenny could still remember her dismay at seeing him go.

She could remember his words. 'We're adults, for God's sake. If you really loved me, Jenny, you'd behave like a woman.' And he had been too angry to listen to her protests, had not wanted to understand that all her life she had known she would sleep only with a man whom she loved and when she was married to him.

His words, and hers, had been on her mind when she had left the restaurant after seeing him for the last time. She had wondered whether her reluctance to sleep with Bruce could have influenced his wish to be alone for a while. And even while she had questioned if she had behaved foolishly—for there was truth in his words, they were adults and she loved him—she had known that there must be more to his decision than that.

But it was not the moral rightness of her behaviour after the dance which came to her now, as she drove a silent Joshua through the game park. Nor did she dwell on Bruce's reasons for going away. Her mind was on the emotions she had felt when Bruce had made love to her. There *had* been enjoyment, but the excitement that had stirred in her in those few seconds when her body had been close to Joshua's, that was something new. It was an excitement she had never experienced before.

It was an excitement she did not wish to experience again, she told herself. At least not with Joshua Adams, a man who had re-entered her life abruptly, and who would leave it just as abruptly when he had concluded his business.

She was driving very slowly. There was a twenty-five-mile per hour speed limit in the game park, but to see game it was necessary to drive even more slowly. The straight sand road required little of Jenny's concentration, so that it was easy for her to glance aside at her silent passenger.

She could see only his profile. His nose was well shaped, his chin, from the side, had the same strong line as his jaw had full-face. She did not need to see his eyes to know that they were dark and grey and unsmiling. How would he look if he laughed? she wondered. She had seen his amusement, but it had been an amusement tinged with mockery. She had a feeling that he was a man who would be capable of laughter, hearty and genuine, and she guessed that she would never hear it. Laughter was something that Joshua Adams would reserve for certain people, those who were close to him perhaps. For the first time, inconsequentially so it seemed, she wondered if he was married. His hands were bare of rings, but that in itself signified nothing. Joshua was a man who might scorn personal adornment of any kind.

Pushing the thought from her mind, she recalled her reaction on learning of Joshua's importance in her life. There had been apprehension, a strange sense of dread—feelings she had tried to tell herself later were unjustified.

Now, with Joshua in the flesh beside her, she thought that instinct had played her even truer than she had realised. Her initial fears had been for Impalavlei. Memory of an impatient boy coupled with a glimpse of Joshua's handwriting had led her to think that Martin Adams' son might be no easy man to deal with. Those fears still existed—the unsmiling face of the man beside her, and his arrogant manner since coming to the game park, had done nothing to allay them.

But a new fear had been added, one that was totally unexpected, one with which it might be more difficult to cope. It was a fear that rested on an entirely personal level. Abruptly Jenny jerked her eyes away from Joshua and back to the road. She had known the man hardly more than an hour—childhood acquaintance was in this case irrelevant—and already she was letting a dominant masculinity get to her in a most ridiculous manner.

A little way ahead a flash of brown showed through the trees. A kudu, guessed Jenny, with the intuitive powers of one who has lived in the bush a long time. Glad of a distraction for her thoughts, she drew the car to a halt alongside a clump of leafy acacias.

For a few seconds there was only the dust the car had stirred up, then the dust settled, and the kudu was visible. If the lion was the king of all beasts, then the kudu was surely the king of the antelope, Jenny often thought. This beast was particularly imposing—a kudu bull, with spreading horns and a powerful body with distinctive white lines running along it in rippling stripes. It was nibbling at the leaves of the tree, undisturbed by the dust and the car. Presently it turned, and eyes that were great and black and liquid stared unblinkingly. There was no sense of alarm, no feeling of being in any way threatened. A regal animal, at home in its domain.

'Beautiful, isn't it?' she commented, turning to Joshua.

An eyebrow rose, but otherwise the grey eyes

were impenetrable. 'Very,' he agreed drily.

He was insensitive, Jenny thought grimly, and tried to ignore the feeling of disappointment that the lovely sight should have left him untouched. The kudu was nibbling leaves once more. Ordinarily Jenny would have waited a while, allowing her passenger and herself to savour the sight. As Joshua himself had suggested this drive she had presumed he wanted to see animals. His disinterest came as a surprise.

'I take it you'd like to go on,' she said, very politely.

A brief lifting at the corners of his mouth revealed that her hint was not lost on him. 'Please,' he answered, and his tone was equally polite.

A few miles further on he asked her to stop. Jenny looked around her. There was not an animal in sight. 'Right here?' she questioned puzzled.

'Here,' he assented.

With a slight shrug Jenny drew the car to a halt. In the space of just a few hours she had discovered that Joshua Adams was a man unlike anyone she knew. Bruce had liked to talk. Any action had been explained volubly both before and after the event. In that respect he was much like the other folk who inhabited the world of fashion and interior design. Jenny was accustomed to garrulousness, to reasons and excuses and large doses of drama.

Joshua, it seemed, was a man who was not given to talk when he did not deem it necessary. She had sensed already his strength and self-sufficiency. Joshua Adams' decisions would never be influenced by others. Though Jenny was slightly piqued, she could not help being impressed as well. But if Joshua meant to be uncommunicative she could match him at the game. As she switched off the ignition she was as silent as he was.

They were at the top of a rise. On all sides lay the game park—an endless vista of thorn trees and bush, of dust whirls and rocks where the sun made a dazzle of heat-haze. Overhead the sky was vast and blue, a metallic blue with just a few wisps of white cloud to relieve it. To the naked eye there was no stirring in the bush. Yet to the east, some distance away, a few black specks circled the sky—vultures, Jenny knew, and understood that there had been a kill. In the long dry grasses lay an animal, an impala perhaps, a zebra or a wildebeest, an animal laid to the ground by a predator. When the hunter had finished its meal the vultures would descend. It was a sight Jenny had known from childhood, but it was one which never failed to distress her, and involuntarily she shivered.

She turned once more to Joshua. He had wound down down his window, and his gaze was fixed on the vastness of the veld beneath the rise. Jenny could not see his eyes, but she saw the tautness of the long body, and the alert lift of the dark-haired head. She could only guess at Joshua's thoughts, but there was something in his bearing that she recognised. Just so had her father looked when he had surveyed the bush.

Her father had loved the veld. The game park had been far more to him than a business enterprise. It had been his home, the place which he had loved more than any other.

Jenny did not know how long they sat at the top of the rise while Joshua looked out over a view that was many things; solitude and serenity, beauty and excitement, savageness and fear. She wondered whether the bushveld could possibly mean to Joshua Adams what it had meant to her father. For once Jenny had no eyes for the view. Her attention was on the man at her side, large and silent and disturbing. The lump that came into her throat was unexpected. When he turned towards her, suddenly, she was caught off guard. She could not swallow the lump away, just as she could not stem the tears that had gathered behind her eyelids.

For a long moment his eyes held hers. She wanted to look away from an expression that was different from anything she had seen before, either in Joshua or in anyone else, and found that she could not. It was a strange expression, at once moving and disturbing, the expression of a man who had waited a long while to see one sight, and who had found in addition something more than he had expected.

Then Joshua said, 'Shall we go on?' His voice was dry. Jenny looked at him a second longer before starting the engine once more, and she knew that in a moment of emotion which she did not fully understand she had been imagining things.

They had crossed the bed of a dry river when he asked her to stop again, and once more she was puzzled. It was not the first time she had taken people for a drive. Most were interested only in seeing animals, particularly the larger species of the cat family, lions and cheetahs and leopards, predators that were not easy to find. But Joshua Adams did not fall into the category of 'most visitors'; Jenny had already had ample evidence of that. Why he would want to pause at a spot that was arid and almost devoid of game she could not imagine, but she knew that he would have a reason. Joshua, she sensed, would have reasons for everything he did.

The river-bed was much like the river Jenny had crossed on her arrival at Impalavlei; much like most of the streams and vleis in the game park. The banks were sandy, a soft dry sand pocked with the footprints of the many animals who had come to this spot in search of water. Jenny recognised the hooved prints of impala and kudu, and the human-like marks of baboons. There was the heavy depression of an elephant. The print was old. From George she had learned that it was a long while since elephant had roamed this way.

A little way downstream a few impala scraped at the dusty earth with their feet. Their movements were tired yet frantic, and Jenny watched them sadly. They were digging for the few drops of water that might still be under the sand, she knew. It was a depressing sight.

'It's been a dry year,' Jenny said, almost to

herself, her eyes still on the struggling animals.

She was unprepared for the hand that caught her wrist, bringing her swinging round to face him. There was strength in the grip, a latent savageness. But for the sudden tingling that shot up her arm, she might have felt pain.

Joshua's eyes glinted like polished flint, his expression was angry. He was a very different man from the one Jenny had glimpsed in the moments on the rise.

'So it's been a dry year!'

Bewildered at the biting quality in his tone, she stared at him. 'Yes. There's been no rain . . .'

'In other words, no water for the animals.'

'Very little.' It was hard for her to think while his fingers gripped her. The touch was purely one of anger, nevertheless it was doing alarming things to her pulse-rate.

'What's been done about it?' His words were clipped, precise.

She shook her head a little numbly. 'Let go my arm.' And then, when he'd done so, abruptly, leaving behind an inexplicable emptiness, she said, 'Nothing, I guess.'

The epithet that exploded from his lips was one not normally used in female company. Then Joshua demanded, 'What was your father doing all these years?'

Bewilderment vanished as Jenny's own anger came to the fore. The fact that Joshua Adams had come to the financial rescue of Impalavlei was forgotten as she turned on him, violet eyes blazing. 'Have you lived in America so long that you think you can manipulate the weather? This is Africa, Joshua.'

'So it is.' The gaze that lingered on her face was enigmatic, as if her anger had showed him a new slant on her.

Jenny was beyond caring. 'We have floods. We also have droughts. Both are beyond our control.'

'The events are beyond our control,' he agreed, 'but not the consequences.'

His tone was quiet—just as if he were talking to a naughty child, Jenny thought, one that could be calmed by reasoning. From the moment that he had arrived at Impalavlei his attitude had been patronising. There was just so much that she was prepared to take.

'I don't know what the hell you're talking about,' she blazed at him, 'but I do know you're saying my father didn't know his business. You've implied it ever since you arrived.'

'Perhaps I have.'

'You've no right to!'

'And that's where you're wrong.'

The blood drained from her cheeks as Jenny stared at him. How foolish she had been to forget, even for one moment, that Joshua had the upper hand here. 'You're talking of the loan,' she said at length.

'A loan that was more of a present.' His voice was flat. 'I had an inkling that the game park was being mismanaged, but quite how much I didn't know.' His eyes hardened. 'Small wonder that Tom Malloy couldn't raise finance at a bank. He'd have had no chance to repay it.'

He talked as if he had written off the loan he had made. Unsteadily Jenny said, 'Assuming you're right—and I don't concede that you are—did you ever take up your thoughts with Dad?'

'No.'

'Why not?'

Joshua did not answer immediately. He was studying her again. Jenny did not know the picture she made—violet eyes that were too expressive, and so big that they seemed to dwarf her elfin face: wayward curls that tumbled about her head and to her shoulders despite the attempt to brush them into tidiness; lips that reflected the pallor of her face and which quivered at the corners. She only knew that the scrutiny was more disturbing than any she had ever experienced. Involuntarily she remembered the reaction his hand on her wrist had provoked.

'Why not?' she repeated, not so much now because she wanted to hear the answer, but because she could not endure the stillness that accompanied his scrutiny.

'You know that too. My father was in your father's debt.'

'What happened was a long time ago.' Belatedly she remembered that Joshua himself had come to her father's assistance. 'It was good of you to help Dad out when he needed it.'

'Thank you for the acknowledgment.' Jenny might have taken the words at face value if they had not been spoken so mockingly. 'My father never forgot the debt.'

'An old loyalty,' said Jenny slowly, moved despite his tone. 'But your father died. It was you who handled Dad's request.'

'You were in your father's confidence, then.'

'In most things. I . . . I didn't know about the loan. Daniel Bannister told me.'

'I see.' He was thoughtful. 'Did you feel an obligation to assume your father's loyalties?'

Easily Joshua met the challenge in the violet eyes. 'I think he would have wanted it.'

'That's why you let things slide when you felt they were being . . . mismanaged.' She got out the last word with difficulty.

A lift of the eyebrows was his only answer. Jenny experienced an urge to slap his face, very hard, and to erase the expression of self-sufficiency. But instead, keeping her voice as controlled as she could, she said, 'You came back when you learned Dad had died. Did the old loyalties die with him?'

'If you want to put it like that,' he said.

She had never met anyone quite so direct. In the world in which she moved people dealt in euphemisms, in flattery and in innuendo. Even Bruce, she realised, did not come out directly with his thoughts. We need time to think, he had said, to be apart . . . If he had wanted to end their relationship he had not made it clear.

But this was no time to be thinking of Bruce. The forceful man just inches away from her required all of her concentration. 'You've no feelings at all for me?' she asked.

He took so long in answering that she wondered if he intended to ignore her question. The gaze that swept her, lingering on her lips before descending to the curves of her figure, brought warmth to her cheeks.

'I wouldn't say that,' he drawled at length.

'But we were talking of mismanagement a few minutes ago. Impalavlei is a mess, Jenny. We've been driving for two hours now, and I've seen hardly a sign of water.'

'There's been no rain. I told you . . .'

'And because of that the game is left to starve—or to look for water elsewhere.'

'The Kruger Park,' Jenny said after a moment, uncertainly.

'Or one of the other private game parks. And that's absurd. This is the age of technology. If water doesn't come your way naturally then you must find ways of getting it.'

'Dad respected the laws of nature.' Jenny's voice was low. 'Granted, we've had some dry years. But we'll have rain again too.'

'Poppycock,' Joshua Adams said succinctly. 'And you know it. Almost every waterhole is dry. Only two boreholes on the property. How could that ever be enough?' His tone was flat as he went on. 'No water, no game. Little wonder that Impalavlei is floundering!'

'It's not floundering!'

'Is that why we have only three guests?'

There was an ominous ring in Joshua's tone, and stealing a glance at him, Jenny saw that his mouth was hard, his jaw very firm. She had fenced with him until now. Intuitively she knew that she could not fence with him any longer.

Even more alarming than his manner was the use of the word 'we'. Daniel Bannister had given her all the facts that she needed, and Joshua had confirmed them, yet somehow, until this moment, she had still thought of him as a visitor—a difficult visitor, to be sure, overbearing and arrogant and hard to ignore. With his use of the word 'we' Jenny was jerked into an acceptance of a new reality.

'It's true we only have three guests.' She looked at him with eyes that were big and wide and troubled. 'And the lack of water . . . that's true too. But Joshua, Dad weathered slack times in the past.'

'Not on his own,' came the grim reply. 'There will have to be changes.'

CHAPTER FOUR

THERE was silence after Joshua's words, a silence which seemed to hang like a pall between them. Jenny had never thought of the Land Rover as small, but now it seemed claustrophobic. It was as if Joshua Adams took up all the space, filling the very air with his aura of power and strength and an intoxicating maleness that clung to him like an invisible second skin.

She could see his trousered legs just inches from hers. Even through the fabric their length was visible, as was the muscled tautness. One hand rested on his thigh, the fingers long and narrow, the nails well shaped. It was crazy that Jenny should be aware of such trivia when matters of urgency were being discussed between them—matters which affected her very life—and yet somehow she was powerless to prevent the direction of her thoughts.

With an effort she jerked her eyes from the thigh and the long strong hand and fixed her gaze on the sandy river bank. The impala had given up their struggle and were wandering downstream towards a line of bush. Nothing could make the dainty animals look anything less than graceful, but there was something disconsolate in the way they walked.

Somewhere they would find water, Jenny knew. There were still resources, secret and hidden, perhaps very small. But they must exist, for if they did not there would be no animals at all in the game park. And yet there was truth in Joshua's statements. Her hostility towards the man could not blind her to that.

'What changes?' she asked at last, in a small voice.

'Big ones.' He paused. 'Look at me, Jenny.'

She stiffened, her gaze glued to the empty river bank. She had no choice but to listen, but she had no need to watch his lips mouthing the words.

'What changes?' she asked again, her tone tight and mutinous.

She was unprepared for the hand that went beneath her hair, one long finger reaching forward to her chin, the others resting lightly on the base of her throat. Despite her outrage, Jenny could not move, for the touch of his fingers had sent alarming sensations flooding down her spine.

The pressure of the fingers increased. As they drew her to face him she was powerless to resist.

'Take your hand away,' she managed to whisper.

'Now that I have your attention, certainly.' His hand left her, rippling the swathe of hair as it passed beneath it. Once more, to Jenny's utmost consternation, she felt a feeling of disappointment.

Making her face carefully expressionless, she forced herself to look at him. His eyes were narrowed and watchful beneath the thick winging brows. His lips were just slightly lifted at the corners, as if he understood her effort and was amused by it. His hair was dark and thick and glossy. A wave of it had fallen forward over his forehead. In another man Jenny would have thought that the slight boyish touch gave the stern face a tinge of vulnerability, but there was nothing vulnerable about Joshua Adams, she knew that now.

'Water will be the primary objective,' he told her.

'You'll put down more boreholes, I suppose. Do you know how?' she asked curiously.

'I believe in enlisting experts. We'll fill the dry vleis. Once we have the boreholes we'll find a way of acquainting the animals with their new drinking-places, and the game will return.'

'You leave nothing to chance, do you?' she commented. 'What other changes do you have in mind? I suppose you want to spruce up the office.'

'It should have been done a long time ago. The cost and effort would have been minimal.'

'Anything else?'

Joshua looked at her thoughtfully for a long moment. She did not know why she stirred uneasily beneath his gaze. Then he said, 'We'll renovate the rondavels.' A brief grin showed a flash of teeth against the gauntness of his face. 'You'll be the expert there, Jenny. Tarred roads, of course. A big glass viewing window in the lounge. Better eating facilities.'

She stared at him. For a moment, after he had

fallen silent, she could not speak, then she said, 'You're joking, of course.'

The look he shot her was long and very steady. 'I'm not in the habit of joking about business matters.'

The elfin head swung up. 'That's all Impalavlei is to you. A business!' Her voice was high, taut. 'You come here with your fancy ideas and think you can turn a quiet bushveld retreat into a sophisticated resort . . .'

'Calm down!' he ordered.

'I won't! Who do you think you are, Joshua Adams? Do you think because you once gave Dad a loan you have the right to transform the place that he loved?'

'A very considerable loan,' he said in measured tones.

Jenny bit her lip. 'A considerable loan. You'll get it back.'

Something like admiration glimmered momentarily in the grey eyes. Then Joshua said, 'Brave girl! But foolish too. You've no hope of repaying me.'

Jenny sat up straighter. 'I'll find a way.'

'It just so happens,' Joshua said very softly, 'that I don't want the loan repaid.'

She gaped at him. 'You mean . . . you can't mean you've written it off?'

'Don't be naïve.' The eyes that still held hers were mocking. 'I'm a businessman, Jenny.'

'Perhaps you'd better tell me what you have in mind,' she said quietly.

She thought his eyes softened, but his voice did

not change. 'I intend to build up Impalavlei, make it a game park to be proud of.'

'You want to make it into an American showpiece,' she said.

'I want to make it an African showpiece,' he corrected her. 'I've suggested some improvements. I didn't say I was about to transform a culture.'

'Where do I fit into all this?' It was the question that had trembled on her lips since he had begun to talk of change.

Joshua studied her thoughtfully. 'That depends on you, Jenny.'

Something Daniel Bannister had said came back to her now. It was an option which at the time had seemed unappealing. 'I could put Impalavlei on the market,' she said, striving for a matter-of-factness she was far from feeling.

'No,' softly.

'Daniel Bannister said I could. You'd get what is owing to you. I'd have what is left.'

'Daniel wasn't aware of all the facts.' The softness did not alter. 'He is now.'

Briefly, casually, Joshua explained to Jenny that he possessed the controlling share in the game park. The blood drained from her lips as she listened to him talk, but she did not move. Not by so much as a quiver would she reveal to him the extent of her shock.

Yet perhaps he sensed something of her feelings after all, for when he spoke again it was with a gentleness which she had not thought possible in him. 'As I see it, Jenny, you have two choices.

You can sell your share to me—I'd pay you what it's worth. Or you can hold on to it. You can stay here at Impalavlei, and we could improve the park together.' A slight pause. 'I hope you'll choose the latter.'

Two options that were simple enough on the surface. Yet both were impossible. She could not sell her share of the game park. If the thought of parting with the home she loved had been hard in Daniel Bannister's office, it was more difficult now—for the sale would be to Joshua. The very idea was repugnant.

The second option was no simpler. To remain at Impalavlei would mean agreeing to Joshua's alterations—alterations which were totally against her father's beliefs.

'Well, Jenny?'

He expected an answer immediately. Another measure of his arrogance, Jenny thought, for he had given her no time to consider. Cautiously, she said, 'I take it you want to increase the value of Impalavei. Then you'll want to sell your share.'

'I won't be selling.'

'You won't?' Jenny was incredulous. 'You'll be getting someone in to handle things for you?'

He looked amused. 'Don't you think I'm capable of handling things myself?'

'But you'll be in America.' She wavered. Unaccountably she was unable to meet his gaze. 'You *will* go back to America, of course?'

'Not for the present.' An enigmatic gleam lit his eyes. 'Well, Jenny, *will* you remain here to help me?'

Dazed, she turned away from him. If she remained at Impalavlei, there would be daily contact with Joshua—a contact amounting to a special kind of intimacy. Now there were three guests at the park. At times there were none. Already, in just a few hours, Jenny knew that living with Joshua in the confining limits of the camp would spell ruin for her peace of mind. She could not see him every day, would not . . .

But Joshua, unchecked and unchallenged, would be free to make Impalavlei what he wished. In her mind Jenny visualised what his proposed changes would do to the park. It would change it from a sanctuary of peace and rustic serenity into a model of efficiency; a place of gleaming chrome and gaudy colours, where loud-voiced men and women would come to photograph animals from the picture-windowed convenience of a single viewing point.

Joshua would endow Impalavlei with the qualities Jenny's father had loathed. Of all his suggestions, only the idea of providing water made any sense. And even that would be against her father's beliefs.

Tom Malloy would hate what Joshua intended doing to the property he had loved. Had he been alive he would have fought his benefactor on every issue. Only Jenny could do so in his place.

She expelled a breath she had not known she was holding, and slowly she turned back to Joshua. His eyes were narrowed now, almost as if he knew something of her thoughts. Which was absurd. There was no way he could know.

'I'll stay,' said Jenny.

'I'm glad.' It was said simply, but Jenny noticed that the alertness in the narrowed eyes had not changed.

'Don't be. I'll do everything I can to preserve Impalavlei as it is now.' A sparkle of challenge appeared in the violet eyes. 'And don't think you can force me to leave. I have my rights too, I do know that.'

Bracing herself for a reaction, she faced him, her chin held high, her eyes like polished jewels. She did not know that to the man who watched her she looked like a small ruffled elf.

To her surprise the reaction did not come. All he said was, 'Our association will be interesting.' And then, 'It's very hot here, Jenny. Let's get back.'

By evening Jenny was beginning to wonder whether her decision to stay had been unduly rash. Few words had passed between them during the drive back to the camp. She had kept her eyes on the road with a grim concentration which the low speed limit did not require. If Joshua had talked to her she would have answered him, but she had been determined not to initiate any conversation of her own.

But Joshua had been equally silent. It was as if he had felt that a point had been made and that it did not need further elaboration. In a way his silence had infuriated Jenny even more than his talking would have done, for it had seemed to bespeak a degree of self-sufficiency that was infuriating. The silence had also made her awareness of his physical presence in the vehicle more intense. The man had an aura which was almost tangible. Some women might call it sex appeal, Jenny thought crossly. She herself was not sure what it was, but she did know that it gave her a strange feeling of excitement. She knew too that if this was the effect the man had on her, the further she kept from him the better.

And that was easier said than done. Towards sunset Jenny realised that she would have to ask Joshua to join her for supper. There were no stoves in the rondavels, but outside each one were barbecue facilities built of brick, with metal grids for the meat to lie on. Already the evocative smells of the braaing were beginning to waft through the air; the smells of wood-fire and charcoal and roasting meat. Guests to Impalavlei came prepared. They brought with them as much meat, packed on ice, as they would need for a few days' stay. If they stayed longer, they would drive to the nearest village outside the game park and replenish their stocks.

Joshua would have brought no food with him, Jenny guessed. She had no option but to ask him to join her. He did not appear to be surprised by the invitation, and his acceptance was friendly.

She watched him as he took over the braaing of the meat, turning it on the grid with the easy competence of one who had barbecued many times before. For some reason the sight was annoying. Barbecuing was easy enough, but Jenny suspected that Joshua's competence was symbolic. In her eyes it became a threatening thing. Intuitively she knew that Joshua would show competence in most matters that affected his life. That being the case it would be harder to fight him. And fight him she must if she was to preserve what she had come to think of as the soul of Impalavlei.

It was almost dark when they began to eat. A kerosene lamp hung from a tree above them, shedding light on the table and creating a pool of isolation from the rest of the camp. A stranger seeing them together might have been forgiven for thinking that there was harmony between them, Jenny thought, as she watched Joshua nursing a beer across the table from her. They could even have been taken for husband and wife. She sat up with a start, and wondered how such an idea could even have entered her mind. Thrusting it aside, she saw that Joshua's eyes were averted, making it safe to study him.

The strong chiselled lines of his face, which in daylight made him a man to be respected and reckoned with, were mellowed now. The glow of the lamp softened the planes of the gaunt face, giving it a look of calmness and serenity. But the flickering light played a deceiving game, Jenny knew, for there was nothing either calm or mellow about Joshua Adams. In her mind he had become the enemy. Even now he could be thinking of ways to transform Impalavlei. If she was not careful he would change it so much that nothing of its essential character would remain.

As if he sensed the drift of her thoughts, he spoke into the silence. 'A restaurant.'

'What!' So great was her outrage that Jenny half rose from her chair. 'What did you say?'

'We'll build a restaurant.'

'With neon lights and plastic-topped tables and a juke-box?' Her voice rose with unaccustomed bitterness. 'What a fantastic idea, Joshua! I can't believe Dad didn't think of it years ago.'

'For such a small girl you're extraordinarily uptight.' His voice was low and quiet in the darkness. 'I throw out one small spark of a suggestion, and you react as if I'd exploded a fire-cracker. What's so terrible about a restaurant?'

'Everything!' Jenny gestured helplessly. 'I shouldn't have to explain.'

'Do so anyway.'

'It would destroy the whole atmosphere of the game park.'

She stopped, searching for words, and was glad that Joshua did not interrupt her. When she spoke again her voice was calmer. 'Impalavlei is like an outpost on the fringes of civilisation. It's a place where people can still experience simple pleasures.'

'Like burning their fingers while roasting meat because they came back to camp too late to get their cooking done before dark.'

'It's not like that.' It was only with effort that Jenny kept her voice even, for she had the feeling that Joshua Adams did not respond well to excitable females—at least not where business was concerned.

'Our guests enjoy camp life. Most of them live in big cities. Johannesburg, Pretoria . . . Some even come from as far as Durban. Impalavlei is very basic, I grant you that. It doesn't have the modern conveniences that some of the other parks have. The Kruger Park . . . But it's what people want, at least for a while . . .'

Again she stopped. Her father could have put it so much more eloquently than she did. She could see him, sitting in his camp-chair at twilight, gazing across the river to the miles of veld where his beloved animals roamed. What for his guests was just an interlude, a rustic break in their busy lives, had been for him a philosophy, almost a religion, the only way of life.

Presently she said, 'It's hard to explain. Your father understood it, Joshua, just as mine did. Somehow . . . somehow I'd have thought you'd understand it too.'

'I do understand. That's why I'm here.' She heard the new inflection in his tone. Despite herself, despite all she knew about him, for just a moment she was moved. It was a moment that seemed linked to the one earlier in the day, when they had stopped at the top of the rise and Joshua had let his eyes sweep the veld.

When he spoke again the special note was gone. 'I understand everything you say, Jenny. But did it ever occur to you that there are things that could improve Impalavlei without destroying its character?'

A hand reached across the table to cover one of hers, and the tingling it provoked started in her fingers and shot through her palm to her wrist. Instinctively Jenny tried to pull back her hand, but Joshua's grip tightened.

'We've got off to a bad start, you and I,' he was saying. 'There's no reason for all this hostility.'

All the reason in the world, said a voice inside her, but the physical reaction he had created in her was still so great that she could not say the words out loud.

'Essentially we have similar feelings about Impalavlei,' he insisted, just as if he had heard her protest. 'We just see things differently. I don't believe people would object to change. Adequate water would mean increased game—even you can't tell me we saw many animals this afternoon. A brighter office would give a cheerful first impression. If the furnishings in the rondavels were gay and modern they wouldn't rob the camp of its atmosphere.'

'Let go my hand!' Jenny ordered through clenched teeth.

'As you wish,' he said, and she heard the bubble of laughter in his throat as he released her.

Strangely it required concentration to listen to his words even after the physical contact had been severed. It was as if he was possessed of extraordinary powers, she thought wildly, which could reach out and touch her even when they were quite apart.

The restaurant he envisaged did not resemble the garish picture she had painted, he said. It would be small and intimate, its furnishings in keeping with the rustic atmosphere of the game park. Those of the guests who wanted to barbecue their own meals would be as free to do so as before. But there could be others who would be glad of the facilities a restaurant offered.

As for tarred roads, Joshua did not understand her resistance. The dust kicked up by cars was a nuisance. An animal could be by the roadside, but by the time the dust had cleared it might well have vanished from sight in the bush.

'Tarred roads in a wilderness,' Jenny said tightly. They were words she had heard her father use.

'Why not?' Joshua's tone had remained quiet as he refused to be drawn by her sarcasm. 'I seem to remember that the Kruger National Park wasn't harmed in any way when the roads were tarred. If anything, visitors were glad not to cough up the dust of the cars in front of them.'

She had only to raise an objection and he had an answer. Always one that was reasonable on the surface. Jenny looked across the table at the long lean face, and wondered despairingly how she would find a way to fight him. An idea came to her, quite suddenly. It was not an answer in itself, but it filled her with hope nevertheless.

'All these—improvements—of yours,' she asked, 'have you thought just how much they'll cost?'

In the light of the kerosene lamp she saw him smile. 'I never embark on a business venture without knowing pretty well what I'm in for.'

For a moment she stared at him outraged, then she leaped from her chair. 'A business venture!'

she flung at him, as she moved wildly from the table. 'That's all Impalavlei is to you!'

'Jenny! Don't be a fool.' Again his hand seized her wrist, roughly now, in an effort to force her back into her seat.

This time anger lent her strength. In a quick movement she jerked herself free. 'Just leave me alone, you swine!' she said through her tears. If Joshua answered her she did not hear it as she fled into the night.

CHAPTER FIVE

Had she been able to, Jenny would have run a long way. Anything to put distance between herself and the man who in just a few hours had been transformed from a boy who had hardly featured in her memory into a man who was nothing short of an enemy. However, there was a limit to how far she could go. With the approach of night it was not possible to leave the camp. There was never a time when one could travel the roads on foot, for predators were a constant danger, but in the dark one could not even travel the roads by car. There were no street lights at Impalavlei. Here, as in the great Kruger National Park, it was a rigid rule that no cars could be outside the camp at night.

Jenny had to content herself with a spot near the river, a small stone wall a few feet from the camp fence. As long as she could remember the wall had been a favourite place. Here she had come whenever she had wanted to be alone. She had rested against the hard stone, baking hot sometimes from the rays of the sun, and had gazed unseeingly into the bush as she dreamed of the shape her life would take. Here too she had come when she had been upset or unhappy. The solitude of the place had helped then to put any problems into clearer perspective.

Quite instinctively, she came to the wall now. Though the sun had vanished, the stone still retained some of its daytime warmth. Gratefully Jenny leaned against it, letting the warmth seep into her cold body.

The coldness had been with her for hours; since her first glimpse of Joshua Adams and the realisation of the threat that he posed. He had spoken of a business venture. His tone had been quiet, reasonable; his words had had a ring of doom. Her beloved Impalavlei, the place which through the years had been home and sanctuary and haven, was to Joshua Adams nothing but a business venture. It was a fact that was not to be endured—yet must be. For the galling reality was that Joshua Adams seemed able to call the tune, at least for the moment.

A little way to the left, just beyond the fence, something stirred. A meerkat perhaps, the small rodent-like animal that lived in the bush. Hearing the sound, Jenny felt a relief from her tension. She was letting Joshua Adams get to her in the most absurd way. She was forgetting that Impalavlei was still her home, that however arrogant or domineering Joshua was, he could not rob her of her love for the place. Unless she let him do it.

Leaning forward, she stared thoughtfully towards the blackness of the river.

In the daytime the bush often appeared hushed, silent. At night it vibrated, with a life of its own. It was alive with the murmurings and scufflings of small animals, while now and then the cry of a larger animal rang through the air.

Jenny could understand the fascination the bush had held for her father. It was a place of magic and mystery, of cruelty and beauty. A place where nature took its own course, as it had done for centuries.

There was a sudden low trumpeting. It was like thunder, an awesome sound, echoing in an endless call across the veld. An elephant, Jenny knew, thrilling to the sound as she had always done. And yet she felt sad too, for the sound came from afar. The elephant was in one of the neighbouring game parks, having found some terrain perhaps where water was more plentiful.

Inevitably her mind went back to the afternoon and the drive with Joshua. With an effort she pushed the memory away—she would not let the man dominate her private moments—and forced herself to dwell on other things.

The vibrant bushveld night was conducive to memories. Almost too much so, Jenny realised, as one memory after another washed over her in a wave of nostalgia. Her childhood happiness, rent with grief at the sudden death of her mother in a car accident. The closness with her father—a closeness which had not lessened when she had left Impalavlei to take up her career in Pretoria.

There were other memories too—Bruce, and a love which she had thought was beautiful and secure; a love which now seemed very fragile. Notwithstanding that Bruce had said all they both needed was time to be alone, Jenny doubted more and more that there was a future left for them. Even if he still thought in terms of marriage, she was no longer certain that it was what she wanted.

Vaguely she knew that her feelings were connected with a new awareness that what she had felt for Bruce might not have been love at all, but could well have been nothing more than a great affection. She had never thought that she could be more than pleasantly stirred by a man. The last hours had revealed otherwise. Joshua Adams had aroused in her sensations that she had not experienced before. She did not like Joshua, in fact she wasn't sure when she had felt quite so antagonistic towards a man; nor was she sure that she had liked the sensations that his touch had provoked. Nevertheless she could not discount them. Much as she had enjoyed Bruce's kisses, she had never experienced anything similar with him. Perhaps the time to ask herself why was now, before Bruce reappeared in her life.

Again she thrust Joshua from her mind. If anything she disliked him more now than before. It was not enough that he meant to ruin Impalavlei, with the compelling force of his personality he had intruded into her personal life as well.

She was filled all at once with sorrow. Too many memories could bring that on, she thought. She had not meant to dwell on the unexpected turn her life had taken, but by trying to push Joshua from her mind she had done just that. Two months ago she could not have visualised herself alone at this wall, staring into a bushveld night. Her father had been alive then. Bruce had been an integral part of her evenings and weekends, while the decor of the penthouse had occupied her working hours. Marriage had been definite, not too far in the future though no date had been planned.

In a few days all had changed. The decision to return to Impalavlei had seemed the correct one. The homecoming had been as happy as it could be with the loss of her father still so recent. Little had she imagined that the homecoming was to be filled with conflict. For she had no doubt at all that conflict lay ahead.

Nostalgia had brought her close to tears. Unexpectedly she felt them spill on to her cheeks. Without quite knowing what she cried for, she let them fall unchecked. She was alone, and it was dark, and weeping brought its own release.

'Jenny . . .'

Involuntarily her head swung round. Then back just as quickly, to hide the tears. It took a second for her to realise, gratefully, that he could not see them. She herself could make out no more than a tall figure, sinuous as a jungle animal in the half-light. It was too dark to make out his features. With a sense of shock she realised that she did not have to see them; they were etched quite clearly on her mind.

Keeping her voice very low, she said, 'Leave me alone.'

'When you've told me why you're crying.' His tone had the gentleness she had heard in it once or twice.

'I'm not crying.'

As he came nearer and leaned against the wall

just inches from her, she heard him laugh. The sound was low and amused and infinitely seductive. Jenny suppressed a quiver.

'That's one point I've learned never to argue about with a female. Do you have a handkerchief?'

She shook her head.

'Fortunately I have,' Joshua said cheerfully.

Before she could stop him he was touching her face, a piece of fabric held loosely in his hand. The last time she had had her tears wiped away had been by her mother, a gesture of comfort for a small unhappy girl. There was nothing even remotely parent-like in the hand that moved against her now. If the handkerchief mopped up tears she did not feel it. What she felt was long fingers against her cheek, sliding up and down in a movement that was light and slow and disturbingly sensuous.

Jenny made herself sit very still. Now he would leave her, she thought, as his fingers lifted from her face. She took a breath, then expelled it huskily as the fingers moved to the other cheek. If anything the movements were now more sensuous than before. The tears were forgotten as Jenny was swept by a rush of sensation, a feeling of breathlessness and a strange longing that she refused to analyse.

'Leave me,' she managed to whisper.

His only response was to let his thumb trail up towards her ear, and then down, very slowly, to a point at the top of her throat. Till that moment she had not even known it was sensitive.

The caressing fingers bespoke an expert with women. Joshua would know how to arouse any woman, Jenny thought. And it was evident from his words that he had had much opportunity with women. Involuntarily she wondered how many other tears he had dried, the long fingers trailing on soft cheeks in a manner calculated to inflame the senses. The thought brought an odd stab of pain.

A moment later she was aghast, more with herself than with Joshua. What could it possibly matter to her how many women there had been in his past? In his present . . . Her life had enough problems. She dared not let her emotions become involved in a new set of complications.

'Did you follow me?' she asked, more to break a silence that was loaded with an unbearable tension than because she needed to know the answer.

'No.'

She was curious. 'How did you find me in the dark?'

'I knew where to come.' The fingers had not ceased their movement. 'This was your special place when you were little. I figured it might be so still.'

Astonished, she tilted her head back to look at him. 'You can't mean you remember?'

The hand moved lower over her face. The handkerchief had vanished without Jenny's noticing it. Any pretence of wiping away tears had gone. Now a finger was stationary beneath her chin while a thumb made a tantalising track down the slender column of her throat, lingering when it came to the hollow where the pulse was beginning a rapid beat.

'Joshua . . .' Jenny whispered.

'I remember many things,' he said softly.

The statement sounded odd from his lips. For memory implied a past, in this case Joshua's boyhood. More than ever, it seemed to Jenny that this tall lean man with the arrogant bearing and the seductive manner had no connection at all with the boy who had once lived at Impalavlei.

His hands were doing alarming things to her peace of mind. They lingered teasingly at the base of her throat, then edged just slightly beneath the collar of her dress. Bruce had tried to undress her more than once, and each time she had coaxed him out of it. It had not been difficult, she remembered, for she had not had her own feelings to contend with. If Bruce's efforts had gone further, they had nevertheless failed to evoke the erotic sensations which Joshua wrought in her with such ease.

'Why . . . why did you come after me?' she asked bumpily.

'To finish our talk.' His voice was dry.

'We'd finished.' She lifted her hand, and with a swift movement brushed his fingers from her throat. 'There are no more tears, Joshua. And I coudn't bear any more talk about your so-called improvements tonight.'

'I'm not in the mood for that either,' came the surprising rejoinder. 'Jenny, you'll have to stop fighting me.'

'That's what you want to discuss?' And when

he nodded, 'You're crazy if you think I'll stop fighting you! I haven't even begun.'

'You're more like Tom Malloy than I'd realised.' Joshua's tone was light. 'Stubborn, headstrong, clinging to an ideal that's been long outmoded.'

'You don't understand . . .' she began, but he cut her short.

'We agreed not to discuss my improvements. We'll not discuss our attitudes either. At least not tonight.' He paused. When he spoke again his tone had changed. 'Don't fight me, Jenny. We've the makings of a great team.'

'No . . .'

'Yes, poppet. You have spirit and courage and creative ideas—qualities I admire. Let's make a go of it, Jenny.'

She had to answer him quickly. Before the magic of his words coupled with the seductive quality of his tone got the better of her. For one insane moment a wild joy had coursed through her—a joy she managed to suppress with the realisation that his words were nothing but flattery.

'It wouldn't work,' she said flatly.

'I'll show you just how well it would.'

His tone was as mild as before, so that when she felt his arms close around her she was caught unprepared. There was no chance to pull away as he drew her against him and found her lips with his mouth. He had acted so swiftly that she was stunned. As his lips pressed against hers she was limp as a broken doll.

And then the pressure of his mouth increased,

and awareness returned, bringing with it a surge of outrage. How dared he treat her like this! If Joshua thought his sexual expertise was enough to mesmerise any woman to his bidding, he would find that he had made a mistake with Jenny Malloy! Furiously she tried to twist away from him.

With no success. The arms that held her tightened, becoming bands of steel around the slender body. The lips that had been relatively gentle assumed new vigour, crushing down on hers with an insistent hardness that did not allow for escape.

And after several seconds she no longer wanted to escape. That was the appalling thing that she would remember later, when she was alone in the privacy and darkness of her own room. The demanding lips transformed outrage into a shivering excitement. Jenny was no longer thinking when her mouth opened to his, and the kiss became a deep and mutually satisfying experience.

The arms that had been purely a means of holding her to him loosened. One hand slid upward, beneath her hair. The other moved over her back, very slowly, stirring her senses to a madness she had never known before. She could feel him against her, the long lines of his body against the soft curves of her own. The contact had a sweetness which sent her mind whirling.

It was a sweetness which erased the knowledge that this was Joshua holding her, the man she had disliked from the second she had set eyes on him. There was only a female responsiveness which savoured the mobile touch of his lips, and which told her this moment was one she had awaited a long time—all her life, perhaps.

She was arching towards him when he released her. Her legs were so weak that momentarily she swayed. She stared up at him, her eyes unfocused in the darkness. A little of the enchantment still lingered, so that it was not the face of the hateful Joshua Adams that she saw. It was purely the face of a man who had made her feel vital and alive and mysteriously feminine. A long lean face, with strong brows and firm chin, and eyes that were impenetrable.

'Convinced?' he asked softly.

'C—Convinced?'

'That we'd make a good team?'

Reality surged back with his words. Anger too, and an intensification of dislike. 'I'm convinced that you're a swine!' she hissed at him. And for the second time that night she fled from him in the darkness.

In the days that followed Jenny contrived to keep out of Joshua's way as much as she could. She became adept at discovering where in the camp he was busy, and then finding chores to occupy her elsewhere. If Joshua noticed her evasiveness he made no comment. Just as he had made no comment on her flight after their last encounter, or on the smudges beneath her eyes the next morning—smudges which had been etched on to delicate skin by hours of sleeplessness and despair.

After the drive through the game park, Jenny

had understood that the weeks ahead would be difficult. Joshua's lovemaking had revealed that the ordeal was to be even worse than she had imagined. Where previously her concern had been primarily for Impalavlei, now it was equally for herself. The minutes at the stone wall had left her shaken. She had recognised Joshua's immense physical appeal very soon. But she had never dreamed that she could be so affected by it. Particularly when she was still in love—or partly so anyway—with another man.

What was particularly galling was the knowledge that while she had been carried on a tide of sensation, Joshua himself had been merely making use of his considerable expertise to prove a point. At least he did not know that never before had she responded similarly, that no other man had stirred her in the same way. Small consolation, but one she must cling to, for if Joshua were to know the full extent of his impact on her, his superiority and arrogance would know no bounds.

There had been times in the last few days when Jenny had questioned the wisdom of her decision to remain at Impalavlei. There was a part of her that wanted to give up the fight, for she sensed already that it could not be won. Joshua Adams had the air of a man who was able to achieve whatever he set out to do. Financially, as well as in the superior strength of his personality, he seemed to have the upper hand.

Yet Jenny knew that to leave Impalavlei now—for she could offer him her share and he would buy it—would be cowardice. The easy way out. The way of avoiding conflict with a man who was like nobody she had ever met, not only in strength and self-sufficiency, but also in a sexual attractiveness that she might never be exposed to again. Was not sure she wanted to be exposed to . . .

Despite her frail exterior, Jenny Malloy had a stubborn resilience. Having made up her mind that a course of action was the correct one she did not easily change her mind. And she *had* decided that for her father's sake it was important to remain at the game park. She would not change her mind merely because a man called Joshua Adams had arrived on the scene.

Joshua wasted no time putting his plans into effect. Jenny knew that water was his most pressing concern. Experts came to Impalavlei, men with tanned faces and crisp safari suits. Joshua drove them through the game park in the Land Rover, and afterwards there were discussions on the shaded verandah overlooking the river.

Jenny was invited to join in both the excursions and the discussions. Her inclination was to refuse. Not that she disagreed with Joshua's view that water was of paramount importance. She was sensible enough to know that what he said was true. It was his motivation which she suspected. Joshua, Jenny thought, needed water to lure game which in turn would lure more tourists, thus making Impalavlei an attractive business proposition. If he had said that he cared solely for the plight of the animals themselves she would not have believed him.

What she did know was that it was important to be in on what was happening and so she accepted his invitations. She accompanied the men on their drives through the park, and listened to the suggestions they made. Now and then she inserted a comment of her own. Afterwards, her eyes would go to Joshua, of their own volition, so it seemed, and she would notice his gaze resting on her face with a thoughtful expression. And for a moment the other men, as well as the concerns of the game park would be forgotten, and she would feel colour wash her cheeks. It was at such moments that she would remember the first evening, when Joshua had come to her at the stone wall and had kissed her and her whole being had responded to him. He had not touched her again, yet the pressure of his hands on her back, and the taste of his lips on her mouth, were as real now as they had been then. She was swept with a sudden wish, perverse and insane, that she could experience it all again.

The few minutes of lovemaking were far from Joshua's mind, Jenny knew. His kisses had been no more than an attempt to wean her from what he regarded as stubbornness. His emotions had not been touched at all. Jenny detected no change in his expression when he turned his gaze from her back to his advisers.

For a while she would try to concentrate on the discussion, but gradually her attention would wander from the talk of boreholes and expenses and the various methods to be considered. Instead she would find herself watching the faces of the men as they conversed—Joshua in particular. And it was then that she noticed something odd. The faces and the voices of the experts blurred into one indistinguishable mass; Joshua stood apart. She only noticed the other men in so far as they compared to him. A comparison which confirmed her suspicion that Joshua was unlike any man she had ever known. *Above* all others. The difference was there in the proud tilt of the well-shaped head, in the lines of the long body, powerful even when he was relaxed. It was there in the alertness of the dark eyes, in the low vibrance of his voice, in the quiet ease of his own comments and questions. Her observations gave her an inexplicable sense of pride. At the same time they gave her no joy.

Later, when the men had left Impalavlei, Joshua would ask Jenny her opinions. She answered him as well as she could, for to do otherwise would have seemed childish. And she knew already that it was vitally important to her not to appear childish in Joshua's eyes. Making her tone low and matter-of-fact, she tried to match his own. She kept to the topic in hand and did not allow the conversation to veer to a personal level. And when she saw his eyes on her face, narrowed and watchful and with an enigmatic expression that was becoming familiar, she did not let her own eyes shift away.

She was standing at the stone wall on another warm evening when he came to her. Dusk was approaching. Trees and bushes had thrown shadows on the ground. When the elongated shadow of the man appeared and merged with the others on the sand, Jenny did not move. She did not need to turn around to know who was there. Only one person carried quite this atmosphere with him, so that the very air seemed to crackle when he came near.

He stopped still beside her, and leaned his back against the wall. She did not look up at his face, she saw only the long legs stretched out in front of him, one crossing the other at the ankles. He was wearing shorts, and his legs were tanned and muscular. As a shiver rose inside her, she averted her head and stared fixedly into a stretch of veld where a single giraffe was moving through the trees, a slow graceful figure on its way down to the water.

'Hello, Jenny.'

'Hello.' She did not turn.

'Enjoying the view?' She heard the amusement in his tone. He knew the effect he was having on her, she thought furiously.

Her own voice was cool as she answered him. 'Very much.'

'You'll enjoy it all the more when you come back to it.'

She stiffened. 'I'm not going anywhere.'

'You are.' Precise, unquestioning.

Despite herself, Jenny jerked around and lifted her head. The setting sun had caught his face, making it a sculpture of strongly-chiselled bronze. He was an artist's dream, she thought, seeing the well-drawn lines and planes, the jaw that betokened firmness of purpose, the lips that were relaxed and sensual.

'Another drive with the advisers?' she asked, knowing intuitively that he had something else in mind.

'You and I alone.' Joshua paused, as if to heighten the suspense. 'We're going to Pretoria.'

CHAPTER SIX

'YOU'RE crazy!' she burst out.

'We leave tomorrow,' he said, as if he had not heard her. 'Be ready at six.'

'You're crazy,' she said again. And then, 'Why?'

He grinned, his teeth flashing white and strong against the tan. 'A shopping expedition,' he said.

'A long way to go to do some shopping.' Jenny was unable to prevent a sudden breathlessness in her tone.

'We'll be spending the night there.' A sardonic smile.

Jenny's heart began a sudden wild hammering. Just the thought of two days away from the game park in Joshua's company was enough to send excitement coursing through her. And then her eyes met his, and she remembered that he was her adversary. Strange that she could forget the fact even for a second.

Digging her nails hard into the palms of her hands, she said, 'I was right, you really are crazy. And I won't be going.'

'Don't you want to know the purpose of the trip?' His tone was polite, dry, but there was a gleam in his eyes; she had not been abe to hide her moment of excitement from him, she knew.

She bit her lip. No, she wanted to say, I really

don't care a damn. But it was impossible to get the words out when in fact she cared almost too much.

'Let's hear it,' she ventured, as casually as she was able.

'It's time to get the rondavels and the lounge furnished.'

'They are furnished.'

'Shabbily.'

They had had this discussion before, but had not returned to it. The question of water had come before everything else. The establishing of boreholes was now under control. It was time to progress to other matters.

Two weeks ago Jenny would have rejected the idea out of hand, but experience had taught her that this did not work with Joshua. Carefully she asked, 'What exactly do you plan to do?'

'Total renovation.'

Nails dug harder, hurting the softness of her hands. 'Our accommodation has always suited our guests.'

'It won't suit the guests I have in mind.'

She could be provoked just so far before losing her temper. 'You'll turn Impalavlei into an American showpiece,' she accused, not for the first time.

'With your help I won't.'

Caught by something in his tone, her head jerked up. His lips were curved in the hint of a smile, in his eyes was the enigmatic light which she found so disturbing. He was flattering her, she thought. Then could not resist asking, 'What could I do?'

The curve of mobile lips tilted farther. 'A strange question, coming from an interior decorator.'

'I don't consider the rondavels need improving.' If only her tone held more conviction.

'New furniture,' said Joshua. 'Beds, of course, comfortable chairs, chiffoniers, a few new pictures.'

'This is supposed to be a rustic camp, for God's sake, not a plush hotel!'

'Curtains, bedspreads, carpets.' Joshua was relentless.

The words were evocative, conjuring up images of the things she loved—textiles, colours, the feel of good wood beneath her hands. Jenny felt like a gourmet with a superb meal just out of reach.

'Dad will turn in his grave,' she said weakly.

'Be ready at six.' His voice had a satisfied ring.

It was the satisfaction which got through to her. His victory had been so easy, and so assured. All he had had to do was exert his male charm—he must know by now that she was not immune to it—and bait her with a treat she could not resist.

'You're a bastard, Joshua Adams,' she said bitterly.

'And you, Jenny Malloy,' he replied in a tone which she had never heard before, 'are a very beautiful girl without the courage to follow your instincts.'

She would not ask him what he meant. She was

not up to coping with the consequences which would follow such an invitation. Trembling just a little, she turned away. Later, when she had her emotions under control, they could talk again; she would ask him what plans he had for the journey. But at this moment it was important to get away from a presence that was too overwhelming.

'Scared?'

The quiet taunt followed her. Jenny took a breath, then lifted her head and turned back. 'We'd said all that was necessary,' she said disdainfully.

'Had we?'

Joshua reached for her hand, drawing her to him. His grip was gentle, yet she acquiesced. He was like a magician, she thought despairingly, weaving spells, bending her will with the exquisite pleasure of his touch.

'Why aren't you married?'

The question was so unexpected that she tilted her head back to look at him. The sun was lower now, but the last of its rays still warmed his face. He was so near to her that she could see the tiny lights that glinted in the grey eyes, and the myriad laughter lines that made up the two clefts which ran from the corners of his nose to his mouth.

'Why do you ask?' she whispered.

'Because you're very lovely. And there's something incongruous about your living here all alone.'

He was so close to her that the male smell of him filled her nostrils. For a moment she felt quite dizzy. His shirt was open, and as her eyes left his face and descended to his throat she saw the strong thrust of it, and further down the little hairs that curled at the top of his chest. A wave of longing swept her, a longing to be against him, to be kissed by him as she had been once before at this wall. Unconsciously she swayed towards him. And then, as she heard his hiss of breath she looked up again and saw his eyes. The expression had changed. He knew that she wanted him to kiss her.

Stiffening legs that were like water, she took a step away from him. His facial expression had rescued her just in time. She knew already that if he understood the full extent of his power over her he would become totally impossible. She had to disillusion him now, quickly.

She bent her head back even farther, so that he could see her face fully. Then she smiled, a brilliant smile, consciously dazzling, one that was quite foreign to her.

'I'm engaged to be married,' she said.

She remained smiling as she watched his lips tighten and a little muscle work momentarily in the long line of the jaw. The words had made their impact, she thought, and did not know that Joshua was seeing not only her smile, but through it to the tension and hunger in the violet eyes.

'So,' he drawled lazily after a moment. 'Who is the man?'

'His name is Bruce.'

'Where does he hide out?'

He was watching her closely. It was an effort to retain the smile. 'Mostly Pretoria. At the moment he's away on an assignment—he's a photographer in the fashion world.'

Now was the time to change the subject, to break away from his physical hold. The muscles of her face tingled with strain, and she did not know how much longer she could keep up the pose.

As if he anticipated her thoughts Joshua's grip on her wrist tightened. 'Why aren't you with him?'

'I was needed here . . . You know that,' she said helplessly.

'The call of duty, which you answered.' She could feel his breath on her cheek. It was warm and clean. 'He didn't mind you coming here alone?'

The innocuous tone caught her off guard. 'Of course not!'

'Then he's a fool.' Joshua's voice was laced with sudden contempt. 'Doesn't he love you?'

Jenny flinched as the question hit a nerve that was still somewhat raw. 'Of course he does.' She hesitated just a fraction too long. 'And I love him. Separation does no harm when two people love each other.'

'Is that what you believe?' A new seductive quality came into his tone, sending sudden fire through Jenny's veins. 'So your Bruce has complete trust in his lovely fiancée alone in the bushveld.' He drew her even closer. 'Shall we put it to the test?'

She sensed rather than saw the dark head descend. She opened her mouth to voice her protest, but his mouth had covered her parted lips before the words could emerge.

For several seconds she tried to resist him. It was a thought she clung to later. She tried to close her lips against his, but easily he kept them open. His kiss was possessive, demanding, drinking fully of the sweetness of her mouth.

Jenny's hands had formed tight clenched balls which she had pressed between herself and Joshua, pushing against his chest in the hope that he would let her go. But his mouth was her undoing. Her legs were weak as she was invaded with a searing longing. The clenched hands straightened to lie flat against his chest, the fingers spreading over his shoulders, the thumbs finding the patch of bare skin where his shirt was open.

As if he sensed her change of mood and was affected by it, Joshua shifted his hold. As his lips began a new trail of kisses, over her throat now and up towards her ears and her eyes, his hands moved over her back, pulling her towards him at the waist, welding her against him as easily as if she had been a doll made of cloth.

The small slender body was a mass of fire and weakness. Mindlessly she pushed up her hands and wound her arms around his neck, one hand knotting in the thick dark hair above the edge of his collar. His mouth came back to hers, and this time she was kissing him back, hungrily, unthinkingly, recognising only that for the moment this was the sole reality.

When at last they drew apart, like two drowning people gasping for air, she stared at him through passion-glazed eyes that could distinguish no features. It was then, suddenly, that the other reality came back. Bruce . . . The needs of the game park.

When his mouth came down again she was ready for him. 'No!' She twisted away. 'I don't want to.'

His laugh was a little ragged. 'Liar.'

'No.' A half-sob. 'What happened . . . I didn't think . . .' Blindly she pushed away from him. 'Let me go,' she choked.

'You want it as much as I do, Jenny.'

'I don't!' Her head came up and she looked at him wildly, unaware that it was just light enough for him to see the tears that streaked across the small elfin face.

'You shouldn't have kissed me—not like that. And if you dare say a word about Bruce, and trust, I . . . I think I'd kill you!'

To his credit he recognised her distress. There was no taunting rejoinder, no reference to her passionate abandonment. As she moved away from him he said only, 'Six in the morning, Jenny.'

She was several feet away from him when his added words wafted through the still air. 'Sleep well, poppet.'

She would not go with him. Not after what had happened. He had taken advantage of her once, there was no reason to suppose he would not do so again. She could not trust him. A small voice, which she tried in vain to block from her consciousness, told her that she could not trust herself either.

Now, when it was too late, she recalled her resolve not to let Joshua know his impact on her. It was humiliating to remember with what speed that resolve had crumbled. The tantalising expertise of his lips and hands had reduced her to pliant putty.

More humiliating than anything else was the realisation that her body had betrayed her. Twenty-three years old, and priding herself on a sane and firm and common-sense approach to life, Jenny would not have believed that her senses could take precedence over her mind.

It was all a matter of physical attractiveness, she tried to tell herself. Chemistry. Sex appeal coupled with a man's amazing awareness of a woman's deepest needs. That was all there was to it. Joshua was an attractive man who had come into her life at a point when she had been more ready for him than she had realised. Her treacherous senses could as easily have betrayed her with anyone else.

What had happened had nothing to do with love. Love . . . The very word was repugnant in connection with Joshua. If he could set her on fire, he was nevertheless an adversary, a man with superficial ideas and a sense of values very different from her own. It was impossible to love such a man. Besides, no matter that Bruce had chosen to go his own way for a while, she still loved him. Surely she did . . .

She would *not* go with Joshua, she determined, as she closed her eyes and felt herself drifting towards sleep. She would break the news to him when he came to call her. He would be away two days, at least. Two days in which she could enjoy the solitude of Impalavlei. The very bliss her shattered nerves needed.

When the knock sounded at her door just after six, she was ready. She did not know when she had changed her mind, did not want to think about it. And yet, as she took a last look in the mirror, she was glad that she had chosen to wear her dove-coloured slack-suit with a royal blue blouse. One of her favourite outfits, it set off her slender figure to advantage. It was businesslike too, she assured herself hastily.

As she opened the door and Joshua's eyes swept her appearance, she saw a glimmer of approval. And then, as he looked at her face, she saw understanding as well. He knew the mental conflict she had experienced after leaving him last night. Her cheeks warmed beneath his gaze, and she bent quickly, making a pretence of checking the clasp on her overnight bag. By the time she had straightened she had herself under control.

'Good day for travelling,' Joshua observed, squinting at the horizon as they walked to the car, and Jenny took the inconsequential comment for what it was and murmured quiet agreement.

For the second time he had been tactful, she thought to herself, as the car left the camp gates and began its slow journey through the awakening veld. Last night, when emotion had made her particularly vulnerable, he had let the opportunity for a sarcastic comment go by. A few minutes ago he had done likewise. She knew already that Joshua could be ruthless when he chose. That he could also be kind revealed a totally unsuspected side of his character, and the revelation made her feel strangely unsettled.

She kept her eyes fixed on the landscape as the car made its way slowly along the sandy roads of the game park. The half-light of dawn lay over the veld, making slow driving more important than ever. Jenny recalled the agonising sight of a giraffe lying twisted and broken in the road; the result of a fast driver who had failed to see the animal, or perhaps had misjudged its distance from the road in a light which made vision less than perfect. Joshua, she thought, would be a man who could handle speed with easy competence. Evidently he was also a man who respected caution when it was called for.

In the misty light the veld was brooding and mysterious. On the bushes and the leaves of the thorny acacias droplets of dew still hung in webs of shimmering gossamer. Bird-song filled the air, and everywhere there was a sense of expectancy and vitality. A troop of monkeys ran by the side of the road. In the Kruger National Park, where some of the roads were travelled constantly, the monkeys had become used to humans, and would amuse children with their antics as they begged to be fed. But the monkeys which roamed the bush of Impalavlei were shy and fey, and at the approach of the car they scampered into the trees.

In a clearing was a herd of impala. The graceful gazelles were grazing, while a little to one side a stag, the leader of the herd, stood alert and watchful. A few miles farther along were several wildebeeste. The bison-like animals were as unkempt-looking as the impala were graceful. They were like cross old men who had forgotten to comb their hair on getting out of bed, Jenny thought with a touch of amusement. Often where there were wildebeeste there were also zebra. Jenny's eyes searched the bush, but saw nothing.

Joshua was right about one thing, she realised unhappily. There were too few animals in the wide miles of veld that constituted the game park. Though she would not admit it to him, she remembered the times when game had been abundant, when visitors to Impalavlei had had the opportunity of seeing far more than they did now. With any luck, new water-holes would see a return of the animals which had once lived here.

At her side Joshua was silent, but she sensed that his concentration on the awakening bush was similar to her own. She could have told him her thoughts, but she did not. To do so would be to admit that some of his improvements were moves in the right direction. Though she now agreed with him on the subject of water, she would never say so. For Joshua's motives were wrong. He would, she was convinced, never convince her otherwise.

Emerging from Impalavlei, they came at length to the tarred road that led to Pretoria. Still Jenny did not take her eyes from the window. The speed of the car had been accelerated, and Joshua was driving now with the easy expertise she had expected from him.

She wished that she was not quite so acutely aware of him. She had never known that the air could be filled with a tingling that was entirely sexual, but she knew it now. Efficient businessman that he was, Joshua Adams was nevertheless the prototype of the basic man, she thought. There was something compelling about his personality, something earthy and primitive, something which called forth in herself a response that was equally primitive—a response she had never suspected existed. That she should discover it now, with the very man she detested for his manner and his values and his way of thinking, was a fact that was impossible to accept.

She was glad when the city appeared in the distance. The hours of driving had been even more of a strain than she had anticipated. She could stand just so much of being in one small space with Joshua; she wanted to leave the car and take in deep breaths of air, and forget the feeling of restless excitement that coursed through her system.

Pretoria had been transformed in the few short weeks since Jenny had left it. As the car topped a rise she caught her breath at the vista of mauve and green that lay all around and below. The jacaranda trees were in flower, millions upon millions of tiny blossoms making a canopy of sheer loveliness.

It was early spring, and Pretoria was bathed in

the full glory of the blossoms that made it the Jacaranda City of South Africa. At her side, Jenny heard Joshua expel a breath, and knew that he was not untouched by the loveliness. From the height of the rise it was like looking down on clouds of mauve that rippled and shone in the sun.

And then they were driving through the city itself . . . Jacarandas lined the streets and filled the spacious gardens. Beneath the wheels of the car, the fallen petals made a sound like soft rain. By the time Joshua drew to a halt outside one of the city's best hotels Jenny was giddy with beauty.

She came back to earth at sight of the hotel. She was back to the present, to a very cold reality. At least one night away from Impalavlei, Joshua had said. Involuntarily she glanced at him, and saw him watching her, grey eyes gleaming with sardonic amusement.

'Separate rooms,' he informed her.

'Well, naturally, I never thought otherwise.' The voice that was meant to wither was infused with an absurd breathlessness.

The gleam in his eyes deepened. 'Most unnatural, I would say,' he countered with a lazy drawl, and grinned wickedly as she stared outraged. 'Come on, poppet, let's stretch our legs.'

Their rooms were adjoining. Though Joshua had said he would call for her in half an hour, Jenny made no immediate move to unpack. She went instead to the french doors leading out on to a little balcony. Leaning her elbows on the wrought-iron railing, she stared over the city. The view from this point was no less breathtaking than it had been from the hills outside Pretoria. As far as the eye could see the clouds of mauve and green rippled with the wind. Yet Jenny's mood had changed, so that she did not drink in the beauty as she would normally have done.

Just a few feet away, on the other side of the wall, Joshua was freshening up after the drive. She could neither see him nor hear him, yet she was as aware of him as if he had been in the room with her. It was an awareness which disturbed her with its implications.

Glancing at her watch, she saw that some minutes had passed since they had parted. If she wanted to shower and change she would have to hurry. Especially if she meant to look nice. She had a special need to look nice. That too was disturbing.

Joshua did not know Pretoria's shops as she did. He insisted on seeing the best in the city. Despite Jenny's objections to the refurnishing of the camp—she still felt that Joshua would try to attract the type of guest her father would not have wanted—she found herself leading the way to a store that was one of her favourites.

Once there, she was lost in a world that she loved. It was impossible to maintain an air of reserve when all around her was an array of good-quality fabrics. Tentatively she reached out a hand to a length of sea-green sun-filter that was new on the market, and found that quite unconsciously she was assessing its possibilities. It was not the only new material. Jenny drifted from one to another, touching, stroking, testing.

For a while she even forgot Joshua. She was unaware that he stood silently to one side, watching her. She would have been disconcerted had she known that he registered the expressions that flitted across the small expressive face—excitement, wonder, occasional disapproval. She did not know that her eyes had a sparkle, that her lips were parted over pearly-sheened teeth. Nor did she know that to the watching man this aspect of her personality was a revealing feature that he would not have missed.

'See anything we could use?' he asked at length.

'Oh yes!' For the first time, as she turned to look at him, she was smiling, the violet eyes radiant. She registered the sudden tightening of his jaw, but such was her excitement that she gave it no thought.

'Sun-filter is perfect.' A wide gesture. 'Cool colours. Most of the year it's so hot at Impalavlei that we want to create a cool effect.'

He let her talk, let her point out the colours she had in mind, green and blue and turquoise, with splashes of yellow for contrast. If she had forgotten her initial reluctance to co-operate with him, he said nothing to remind her.

They made no purchases. For the moment they were just looking. They went to other departments, other stores. They looked at more fabrics, at furniture, at pictures and ornaments. It would be only later, when Jenny could relive the day in her mind, that she would realise quite how much she had enjoyed herself. How much too she had put of herself into thinking and planning and visualising. She would remember Joshua's comments, would realise that they had been intelligent, showing a grasp of the atmosphere of Impalavlei, an understanding of what would be right for the game park.

Her head was awhirl with all they had seen when Joshua said it was time to call it a day. Tomorrow, when Jenny had had a chance to work on a general scheme, she could make her choices.

It took a moment for his words to make their impact. Then she said wonderingly, 'You're leaving it all to me?'

A long finger reached towards her face. She stood very still as it trailed a path from the corner of her eye down towards her lips. The gesture lasted no more than a few seconds. There was no reason at all for the tremor that shot through her. Somehow she forced herself to meet his eyes, and the smile she saw there made her heart beat a little faster.

'I can think of no better person to leave it to,' he said softly. And then, 'You know the night-spots of Pretoria. Where can we go for a decent meal and some good music?'

CHAPTER SEVEN

IT WAS on the spur of the moment that Jenny had packed the rust-coloured chiffon with the shoe-string straps and the skirt which flowed softly from the fitted bodice. She had remonstrated with herself while she had put it into her suitcase, telling herself that she would have no opportunity to wear it. Now she was glad she had brought it. Her image in the hotel mirror told her that the dress made her look slender and voluptuous and very feminine simultaneously.

It was impossible to stop the small gasp of breath when she opened the door to Joshua's knock. His suit was light grey, the material silky-looking and expensive, the cut faultless. His shirt was a lighter grey, and against it the tanned skin and chiselled features looked more striking than ever. Jenny had thought him good-looking from the first; she had not realised he was quite so distinguished.

The interested eyes of other women in the night-club confirmed her opinion. Jenny did not notice the many male eyes turned her own way. She was in a bemused state that seemed oddly at variance with what was after all only an interlude in a business trip.

Over dinner they talked. It came to Jenny that it was the first time they had talked properly, without verbal fencing and hostility. Joshua had lived so long in America that she had thought he would have forgotten most of his boyhood in Africa, but to her surprise this was not the case at all. He remembered Impalavlei with detail and affection.

He told her a little of his life in America, and of the enterprises in which he was involved. Joshua was a successful businessman, Daniel Bannister the lawyer had said. Jenny had not realised quite how successful he was.

'Are you married?' she asked, and wondered why she had never thought to ask before.

A light smile. 'I thought you knew the answer to that.'

'Why haven't you married?' It was odd how she felt driven to continue the questioning. As she waited for his answer, she remembered that he had asked the same question of herself the previous night.

Eyes that were dark and hard to read in the flickering light of ornamental candles rested on her face, lingered on cheeks that were soft and flushed, on lips that had parted willingly and with abandonment beneath his, then descended to the slender throat and smooth rounded shoulders and the swell of breasts beneath the thin chiffon. Jenny's heart was hammering painfully in her chest, but when Joshua's eyes came up again she met them steadily. 'I guess I just never met the right woman,' he said.

She had to change the subject. 'Why did you come back to Impalavlei?'

His eyebrows rose, and she knew that the moment of emotion—if indeed there had been such a moment other than in her imagination—had passed. 'You know why I came.'

'You could have sent someone else. It was just a loan, after all.'

'It was never *just* a loan. Just as Impalavlei is not *just* an investment.' His tone had altered. 'Impalavlei was my home once, Jenny. I always longed to come back to it.'

'It's not your home any more,' she said unsteadily.

'It could be. At least for part of every year.' He looked at her. 'We have different thoughts about what's right for Impalavlei. We also have something in common. We both regard it as special.'

She wanted to believe him—Oh God, she wanted to believe him! Especially at this moment, when the lines of his face were mellowed in the soft light and his tone had that rare warm ring to it. Jenny remembered the look in his face on the first day, when he had told her to stop on the rise and he had stared out across the bush. It was a moment which had moved her, just as she was moved now.

She wanted to believe him, to trust him. And yet there were things she needed to know before she could give him that trust.

'Why do you want to change the game park?' she asked.

Joshua was silent a long time before he answered. When he began to speak his voice was thoughtful, measured, without a hint of the mockery she so hated. It came to her that this was the first time they had discussed the subject reasonably, without emotion.

'It needs change,' Joshua said at length. 'Your father did a good job, Jenny, but he failed to move with the times.' His eyes twinkled. 'Will you get uptight if I say that Tom was as stubborn as his daughter?'

As recently as last night Jenny would have risen to the bait. She was not quite sure herself why she did not do so now. Perhaps there was a part of her that understood that it would be silly to ruin the evening.

Letting the remark pass, she said instead, 'You were right about the water. But what about the rest, Joshua? This afternoon I was carried away by the colour and fabric, I know that. But is it all necessary? Why do we have to modernise?'

'Because if we don't,' he answered her in measured tones, 'Impalavlei will go on limping along till it comes to a halt.' He shot her a level look. 'How many years do you think it's been since the game park has brought in enough to just come out even?'

His implication was clear. Without his loan—and it was far more than a loan, Jenny understood now—Impalavlei would have been lost to her father long ago.

'You spoke of Impalavlei as home,' she said, the idea coming to her suddenly. 'In that case, does it have to be a going concern?'

'It does,' was the quiet reply. 'It has to pay its way to keep both my love and respect. That's the nature of life, Jenny, whether you want to believe it or not.'

She looked at him helplessly, knowing she could not argue the statement. 'But all this modernisation,' she said at last, uncertainly. 'Does it have to be done?'

'If we're to have more guests, I think it does. Don't equate modernisation with a change in the essential character of a place we both love.' And before she could think of a reply to that he reached for her hand and got to his feet. 'Let's dance.'

The dance-floor was small, lit only by candles from neighbouring tables. As Jenny went into Joshua's arms she was flooded by memories of last night. Then he had made love to her at the stone wall, his lips ravishing her mouth and her face with kisses that were demanding and possessive and destructive to her senses. She remembered the wildness of her responses, the way her body had ached with the sweetness of being near him.

Tonight was different. On the surface it was more civilised—two people dancing, just one couple among a group of people similarly occupied.

And yet in a sense it was not different at all. For with the long male body so close to hers, with the smell of him in her nostrils, and the movements of his thighs brushing tantalisingly against her own, her body was seized with the same wild clamourings as before. As if he understood her reactions—or experienced similar ones of his own—Joshua drew her tighter against him. Now all of her body seemed to have contact with his. The hand that had been holding hers went to her back, both hands sliding high on the bare skin beneath her shoulders. His lips were in her hair, and with a small shudder she let her head rest in the hollow at the base of his throat.

The music was slow, a sensual tune that seemed a fitting accompaniment to her maddened senses. They moved slowly with it, two bodies like one, their feet hardly moving. Jenny thought she could not have danced faster if her life had depended on it. Her head was giddy, her legs like melting wax.

Dimly she knew why she had not argued with Joshua tonight. She had a need for harmony with him, a need for closeness. It was a need that she feared and despised, for it seemed to rob her of all control over her emotions. Yet it was a need which she could no more avoid than she could avoid breathing.

There was a pause in the music. Joshua's hands slid to her waist, lessening the closeness a little. 'Enjoying yourself?' she heard him ask.

She tilted her head back to look at him. He was so much taller than she was that she could not see the expression in his eyes. All she saw was the strong column of his throat, and the long firm line of jaw. But she had heard his voice and knew that he was smiling.

'Very much,' she smiled back at him.

'Then we're friends?'

Oh yes, she was about to say, we're friends.

For the moment at least. And tried to suppress the treacherous inner voice that told her she wanted to be more than just friends.

She was about to answer him when for some reason she found her gaze drawn to the side. She stiffened. Staring at her, with a horrified expression, was Bruce. His arms were around a voluptuous blonde girl, his fingers beneath the fabric of her low-backed dress. The girl's arms were twined about his neck. From the look of things they knew each other very well indeed.

For a very long moment their eyes held, then Jenny saw Bruce swallow hard. A series of emotions flitted across the attractive face—embarrassment, shame, anger, even a plea for understanding.

She stared at him as if at a stranger. If it was forgiveness he sought she could not extend it. Not now. Not with the memory of their last evening together suddenly vivid in her mind.

The band came to her rescue, starting to play once more, another slow melody. Very deliberately Jenny jerked her eyes away from Bruce. As Joshua drew her close, she went to him willingly. Her own arms went up around his neck as her head rested against his throat.

The action was instinctive. She had wanted to prove something to Bruce—her independence, her total unconcern for the way he had treated her. It was an action meant to cover a hurt; it also produced its own consequences.

There was a slight hissing intake of breath just above her right ear, and then she was being welded against Joshua in a closeness that was greater than anything she had experienced. She had thought the previous dance exciting; this one was more so. She was moulded against the long body, in a nearness she could not escape, did not want to escape. It was a nearness which spelled total awareness, which seemed to involve each one of her senses. The beat of his heart was strong and rhythmic; the smell of him was intoxicating. His fingers were tantalising in the way they lay against the soft skin at the top of her back. His legs were instruments of torture, a sweet yet agonising torture, moving against hers with a slow sensuousness that set her body on fire.

Bruce was forgotten. There was only Joshua, only an excitement and an aching need like nothing she had ever known. It was not the moment to question why she felt as she did, nor to try to rationalise that her senses were just a product of some chemical spark. She knew only that she was wrapped in an intimacy that she wished would never end. She knew too that her body was clamouring for a fulfilment which went beyond kisses and dancing.

When the music ended again the band indicated that they were taking a break. Joshua kept his arm around Jenny's shoulders, and she was glad of his support, more than just for the contact it offered. She wondered if he knew that her legs needed time to regain their sense of purpose.

They were about to sit down at their table when a voice from behind them said, 'Jenny . . .'

Turning, she wondered who she could have forgotten the long hard look that had passed between her and her erstwhile fiancé. 'Why, Bruce!' She made her voice as casual as she could. 'How've you been?'

It was impossible not to perform introductions. In the moment that she turned to Joshua she saw his eyes, dark and alert and with the sardonic gleam that she had come to dread.

And then she had to turn back to Bruce once more, and was forced to listen to a discourse of excuses. It seemed that the assignment had ended almost as quickly as it had begun, that he had returned to Pretoria and found her gone, and had not known where to get hold of her. And that, she thought, was not true. Bruce knew that Daniel Bannister was her lawyer, just as he knew that she had gone to Impalavlei.

Once she tried to interrupt him, but it was impossible to stop the bumbling flow of talk. If only he would realise that his explanations were causing her more embarrassment than if he had not even tried to apologise! Was this how relationships ended? she wondered, in some detached and disillusioned area of her mind. And all the while she was aware of Joshua, standing silently to one side, constantly alert.

Bruce went at last. He could not leave his companion alone too long, he said. He had already explained that she was a casual date whom he knew hardly at all. He would be in touch, he said, as he took a step away, and Jenny, smiling brightly, answered, 'That will be nice.'

Dessert had been put on the table while they were dancing: strawberry shortcake topped with whipped cream. As Jenny lifted her spoon, she glanced at Joshua's face. It was set in an expression that was almost deliberately blank. The eyes were inscrutable beneath hooded lids, the jaw looked very firm. Normally she loved shortcake; now she just pushed it about on her plate. Strangely, and for no specific reason, Joshua's attitude was upsetting her more than Bruce's clumsy apologies had done.

It was with a sense of relief that Jenny heard the band strike up again. Dessert finished, she and Joshua returned to the dance-floor, and she went into his arms, moving close against him. One hand went around her back, the other reached for hers. There was not a trace of the contained passion she had felt in him earlier.

Astonished, she tilted her head and looked up at him. She could see his eyes now. He was watching her. He had known she would be surprised, and the upward curve of his lips told her he was amused.

'Disappointed?' he drawled.

She pretended ignorance. 'I don't know what you mean.'

'Sure you do.' His voice was soft, lazy, infinitely dangerous. 'You were hoping for a repeat of the last dance. Sorry, love, but if you want to make your prospective husband jealous you'll play your games without me.'

It was difficult to swallow on the lump at the back of her throat. Bruce's faithlessness had brought some humiliation. Joshua's return to contempt brought sorrow.

As they danced she struggled with her feelings. Joshua thought that she had tried to make Bruce jealous. There was no way she could explain to him that while he was right, the motive had lasted no more than a few seconds. That when she had been close to him in a timeless moment of slow magic and sensation, Bruce had no longer been on her mind. That what she felt for Bruce was no more than hurt pride. That her real feelings were for Joshua, and that they went deeper than words.

She no longer loved Bruce; that much the last minutes had shown. In a sense she had known it for some time. For Bruce had been in her thoughts less and less since her arrival at Impalavlei. She wondered now if what she had once felt for her fiancé had ever been more than a deep affection. Intuitively she understood that if it had indeed been love her reactions on seeing that relationship revealed for what it was would involve more than annoyance and hurt pride.

If only she could rationalise her feelings for Joshua as easily! Something had happened to her in the last days, something powerful and devastating and yet wonderful. Was it possible that she had fallen in love? She fervently hoped that she had not. For loving Joshua would be a very different matter from what had passed as loving Bruce. It would be an emotion which would remain with her long after Joshua himself had vanished from her life.

And vanish he would. He planned to stay quite a long time, he had said the first day. He had not used the word 'always'. Joshua had interests in America. Impalavlei was just another one of his venture. If he regarded it with affection and a sense of being his home—and she thought now that he did—nevertheless the day would come when he would grow restless, when more important matters would call him back to the throbbing metropolis which was his home too.

Perhaps Joshua would remain at Impalavlei for as long as he was needed. Once all the improvements were complete he would move on to other things, Jenny sensed. And most of the improvements were now either planned or under way.

She *could not* let herself fall in love with Joshua. If she did she would be paving the way for eventual unhappiness, and somehow she had to prevent that happening. And yet as she ached to be closer to the strong body, and was consumed with the need to feel him against her once more, she wondered despairingly if it was already too late.

She was glad when Joshua called for the bill. The happiness had gone out of the evening. Perhaps he was as anxious to end it as she was.

At the door of her room she inserted the key in the lock, then looked up. 'Thank you for a nice evening,' she murmured formally.

'To which I'm supposed to say the pleasure was all mine,' he answered, mocking her formality. And then, his hand closing over hers and turning the key, 'As it happens, the evening is not over.'

Deftly, giving her no time to protest, he swung open the door and manoeuvred her into the room. It took a full second for Jenny to realise that he had followed her in and closed the door behind him.

'Get out!' Her voice shook.

'When I'm ready to.'

'Now!' She tried to evade the reaching hands but they were too quick for her. Already the pervading weakness was attacking her body as he drew her close. 'No, Joshua . . .'

'Yes, Jenny.'

'When we were dancing . . . after Bruce left us . . .' It was increasingly hard to speak. Not only was her throat very dry, but she did not know how to put her feelings into words.

'I refused to hold you close.' The statement was cool and precise, but the voice near her ear was disturbingly seductive.

'Why . . . why now?'

His answer was to draw her nearer. When she felt his teeth nibble at an ear-lobe she gave a little gasp.

'Joshua . . .?' A shaken whisper.

His unexpected action had sent a tremor through a system that tonight was extraordinarily vulnerable. The sound of his laugh, low and husky, increased a need that had been a part of her since they had first stepped on to the dance-floor together. Jenny had wanted so badly to have him kiss her, caress her, but now there was also the need to know why he had behaved as he did.

'I never make love on order,' he said, putting

her a little away from him and looking down into her face. 'And that was what happened tonight, wasn't it, Jenny? You wanted to annoy your fiancé—quite justifiably so—and I conveniently happened to fit the bill.'

Jenny remembered the sensual intimacy of their first dance, before she had seen Bruce. But there was no sense in arguing the point. Joshua would not have known when she had spotted her fiancé. He might not even believe her.

Instead, with a provocation she had not known she possessed, she asked, 'When do you make love, Joshua?'

There was a gleam in the dark eyes looking down at her. He had recognised the provocation for what it was. Jenny held her breath.

'When the mood takes me,' came his reply, in a tone that was low and lazy. Long fingers went to the ear he had nibbled, and played with the lobe for a few seconds before drawing a line down her throat.

'When I'm with a woman who's very beautiful. And very sexy.' The fingers lingered on the most sensitive parts of her throat, pausing at last with a tantalising lightness in the hollow where a pulse beat too quickly.

'And sometimes when I'm invited.' Now the fingers moved downwards again, to the swell of breasts above the low cut of the chiffon dress. Jenny tensed as she felt the softness of her body harden beneath his touch. She heard him say, 'As I'm being invited now.'

She did not answer, did not even try to answer.

Even if she had been able to, there would have been nothing to say. The involuntary responses of her own body said it all for her.

He did not wait for an answer, but drew her close once more. One arm was beneath her shoulderblades, the fingers flat on the bare skin as they had been when they were dancing. The other arm supported her neck as he bent her back for his kiss. His lips played on hers, gently at first, then with a growing passion. He wanted her to respond, she sensed, but with the memory of his rejection on the dance-floor still woundingly vivid she kept her mouth tightly closed.

He lifted his head. 'Kiss me.'

'No . . .' It was a whisper.

'Yes,' he insisted. 'You know it's what you want.'

He drew her against him again. This time his lips went first to her throat, igniting a fiery trail where his fingers had been just minutes ago. Jenny lost the capacity to think as shivers of delight coursed through her. Of her own accord she arched even closer towards him, filled only with the need to feel the hard long body against hers. This time when his lips met hers she responded willingly, mindlessly, kissing him back with a fervour she had not even dreamed she possessed.

So erotic was his touch that when she felt his fingers going to her dress she did not immediately register the implications of the zip being pulled down. Joshua loosened his grip on her just long enough to slip the garment from her shoulders in one swift yet gentle movement. Then she was in his arms again, her hips pulled against his, and her breasts hard against his chest where his shirt was now unbuttoned. Had she opened the buttons herself? She did not know. She knew only that the touch of the rough muscled skin against her own tender flesh was a sensual experience that she wanted to prolong.

And then he was lifting her in his arms and carrying her to the bed. He lowered her on to the blankets. She opened her eyes and looked at him. His eyes were on her body, lingering on a narrow waist and a flat stomach and gently curved hips; ascending to breasts that had told him in their own way just how much she wanted him: ascending further, to her face, to lips that were soft and swollen from his kisses, to eyes that were dazed with passion, yet alight with a creeping understanding.

For the first time she had realised that she was naked. Realised also that Joshua was beginning to undress himself. Understood that their lovemaking was about to enter a new dimension.

They looked at each other a long moment. Jenny's throat was so full that she could not speak. Her body throbbed with a need that cried out to be fulfilled. And yet somewhere a remnant of sanity had returned. As she watched him remove his shirt she knew that his lovemaking was what she wanted more than anything in the world. She knew too that she was not ready for it.

She had never thought that she would sleep with a man unless he was her husband. Unless she loved him. Joshua was not her husband, and never would be. Why then this longing that was like a gnawing tangible thing? In the night-club she had told herself that she must not fall in love with Joshua; had wondered also if there was still a way to prevent it.

If she slept with him now she would have committed herself to him totally, not only with her body, but also with her mind and heart and senses. There would be no drawing back, at least not for her. The memory of this one night would haunt her all her life. Through her longing there came a stab of fear.

She was about to speak when Joshua lowered himself on to the bed. As he bent over her and looked down at her body there was an expression in his eyes which she had not seen before, an expression which she had never hoped to see applied to herself, something like awe and reverence. Jenny swallowed hard.

'Joshua . . .'

As if he had not heard the plea in her tone he said huskily, 'My God, you're beautiful!'

'Joshua . . .' she began again, but now he was bending over her, and his lips were on her breasts, following the curve first of one, then the other, then kissing nipples that were hard and rosy. Instinctively Jenny reached for him, burying her hands in the thick dark hair behind his head.

As if her action struck the final spark to his own inflamed feelings, Joshua groaned and sat up.

'I want you, Jenny.' His voice was ragged.

Violet eyes fluttered open, moist and luminous under long dark lashes. As the blur cleared from her vision she saw that he was unbuckling his belt. Another minute and there would be no drawing back. As it was, she might have waited too long.

'Joshua, no!' She lifted herself on to her elbows. 'I . . . I don't want it.'

'You're frightened,' he said soothingly.

Yes, she was frightened. Not of the act itself, for her body clamoured for it. She was frightened of the consequences. Of going through life with the memory of what she had once experienced and could never hope to experience again.

'I'll be gentle,' he was saying. 'I won't hurt you.'

She shook her head. 'It's not that . . .'

He was looking at her, his eyes harder now, his lips tight. 'Don't try to tell me you're thinking of Bruce.'

Her only way out, and she had to take it. For if she told Joshua her true fear he would find a way of rationalising it away.

'Yes.' Veiling eyes that were too easy to read, she said, 'Seeing him tonight . . .'

'He was with another woman,' Joshua said harshly.

'That . . . that doesn't change my own feelings.' Jenny bit her lip. 'I don't expect you to understand.'

'Damn right I don't!' He was furious. 'Why the hell did you provoke me if you didn't mean to go through with it?'

'I said you wouldn't understand,' she ventured nervously.

He had stood up and was pulling on his shirt. At her words he swung round. 'I understand that lovely little body of yours. It cries out to be made love to. I don't pretend to understand what goes on in your mind, Jenny—and after this I doubt that I want to.'

He was out of the room before she could answer him. Not that she could have answered him anyway. When she had heard the violent slam of the adjoining door she pulled the pillow over her head and wept as she had not done for years.

Jenny was glad that the next weeks were busy ones. Within the bounds of camp life it was almost impossible to avoid Joshua completely. But their moments of contact were limited.

Joshua now had his own eating facilities. He did not suggest that they share their meals, nor did Jenny issue invitations of her own. For the rest, their daytime hours were fully taken up with the business of running Impalavlei.

Sometimes at night, when darkness lay over the land and the silence was broken only by the sporadic cries of the animals, Jenny would wonder what Joshua was doing. It was then that she found it hard not to think of him. Acutely aware of his presence in his own room, just a few yards from hers, she would remember the time they had spent together in Pretoria. Much as she tried, she could not push the memories from her—the companionship during dinner, the sensuousness of the dance, the excitement of his lovemaking in her hotel room and her own abandoned responses. And finally, his anger at her withdrawal, an anger which by the next day had turned into a chilling indifference.

An indifference which seemed still to exist, for Joshua never sought her out. Any conversation between them related strictly to Impalavlei, usually to the improvements in process.

The improvements were taking shape with a speed Jenny had not thought possible. Progress had been made on the boreholes, and soon attempts would be made to coax the animals back to their old grazing grounds. Jenny knew that Joshua still conferred with expert veteran game rangers who were able to give him the benefit of their knowledge and experience.

The road leading from the camp to the gates of Impalavlei had been tarred. In time the other roads would be tarred too. This was one improvement which, Jenny had thought, would spoil the atmosphere of the game park, but after driving that way she was no longer sure. When she stopped to watch an animal there was no need to wait for the dust to clear first. But if it was a change for the better she did not say so to Joshua. Besides the matter of his indifference towards her, she thought his self-confidence was such that he needed no compliments to bolster it further.

Everywhere there were workmen. The appearance of the main building had been altered. A picture window took up the entire length of one wall of the lounge, so that what had once been a series of small windows interrupted by columns of brick was now one great expanse of clear glass giving a panoramic view of the river and the bush beyond.

Some way out of the camp a viewing platform was being constructed in the branches of an enormous tree. When Jenny had taxed Joshua with adopting the idea from a famous game reserve in Kenya, he had not denied it. Both the tree and its location near a lovely water-hole were ideal for the project. The platform would be a marvellous place for visitors to sit and watch for game which they might not normally see from their cars.

Now and then Jenny remembered her decision to fight Joshua every step of the way. Wryly she had to acknowledge that the decision had been made at a time when she had not understood the full strength of her adversary. Joshua was no easy man to fight. He knew what he wanted. He knew how to achieve his aims and had the money to finance them. Above all, it did not seem to occur to him that what he did might be ill-judged.

Alone with her thoughts, Jenny knew that there was another reason why she had not fought him. She was no longer convinced that he was in fact wrong. Somehow, without her being fully conscious of what was happening, he must have brought her around to his own way of thinking.

All along she had believed that her father would have hated the changes Joshua had brought to Impalavlei, but now she was no longer certain. If her father had been possessed of certain ideals, he had also been blessed with an open mind. Seeing the game park as it was now, its setting enhanced, its soul intact, he might have been content with the transformation.

There had been a time when she had thought Joshua saw Impalavlei only as an investment. Then he had said he thought of the game park as home, and she was beginning to believe him. For despite her initial doubts, Jenny had to admit to herself that the changes might in fact have been for the good of Impalavlei. If they succeeded in bringing more guests to the game park, the renovations were also in good taste. Impalavlei had not become the gaudy tourist spot she had feared. The essential character and atmosphere of the park had been preserved.

Jenny's task had been to redecorate. The office had been given a fresh look; efficiency combined with a pleasant first impression. The lounge was nearly ready. Here Jenny had given her imagination free rein. When she looked around the nearly-completed room she could not suppress a sense of pride. She had taken advantage of the new brightness provided by the picture window, had taken advantage too of the money Joshua had placed at her disposal—if he did not like her very much, at least he seemed to evidence respect in her judgment.

The old room had been comfortable, shabby and a little dark. The new room was no less comfortable. It was modern and appealing, but in its rustic flavour was not a touch of artifice. Jenny knew it ranked among her best efforts.

Now she was putting the finishing touches to one of the rondavels. In a part of the land where it was almost always hot, Jenny had striven for coolness. Turquoise sun-filter curtains blended subtly with the deeper colour of the bedspreads. On the stone floor was a woven mat. Soft under bare feet, its flashes of yellow provided a touch of cheerful contrast. On the wall was a group of prints. The subject was animals, the drawings cleverly executed with fluid strokes which lifted them out of the ordinary.

Would a guest be happy here? Jenny wondered. On impulse she sat down at the dressing-table. Leaning her chin on her hands, she stared at her image in the mirror. Pleased with her results, she could not help wondering what she would do when her part in the renovation of Impalavlei was at an end.

For no reason at all she thought of Joshua, then realised that no reason was needed. Much as she tried to concentrate on her work, Joshua Adams was never far from her mind.

She heard the door of the rondavel open, and she did not need to turn around to know who had come in. It could have been one of the staff, but the hair that rose on the back of her neck told her it was Joshua. It seemed to Jenny sometimes that he carried his own special aura with him wherever he went.

She remained sitting at the dressing-table, but her chin left her hands as she sat up straight. She heard him stop in the open doorway, then the sound of footsteps as he came near. He had not said a word, nor had she. Inside her the stomach muscles knotted.

And then his face appeared in the mirror. For what seemed like hours, but could have been no more than seconds, two pairs of eyes caught and held in the glass. The violet eyes were wide and startled. The grey ones held an amused gleam. But there was another expression in them also which sent the heart in the small feminine body racing.

'Hello, Jenny,' said Joshua, when Jenny thought she could not take the suspense a moment longer.

'Hello.'

He was very near her. She could feel his peculiar vibrations reaching out to her, could feel the beginnings of response within herself. There had not been an hour since the night in Pretoria when she had not thought of him, and yet, Jenny realised now, the intensity of his maleness was still more overpowering than she had remembered.

She had to lessen the tension. 'Did . . . you want something?

'Yes.' His glance lingered on her face, taking in the sudden warmth in her cheeks; then descended to as much of her body as was reflected in the mirror.

'Among other things,' he drawled, his tone such that she had no difficulty registering the double meaning, 'I wanted to compliment you on your furnishings.'

'You like them?' On a surge of pleasure she half-turned, and found that he was even closer than she had realised, so that her face brushed his thighs. Flustered, she turned back. The gleam in his eyes told her that the increased redness in her cheeks was not lost on him.

'I certainly do.' His hands went to her shoulders. She could feel each one of his fingers. 'Not that I expected otherwise.'

'I'm glad,' she said unsteadily.

'The colours are good—turquoise in this rondavel, lime and blue in the others.' He had taken a step closer, and now she could feel the tops of his thighs against her back. There was a tautness of muscles, a burning warmth that seemed to flow from his body to hers through her thin cotton blouse.

'The office too,' he continued, as his fingers began a tantalising movement over her shoulders and towards her throat. 'It makes a good first impression.'

His words could not have been more mundane. He was making statements which her colleagues had used every day. And yet none of her business conversations had ever been conducted with such sensuousness, she thought wildly.

Nor had they produced a similar response. It was useless to deny to herself her pleasure at his touch. Her legs were like water, her nerve-stream was aflame. She had missed Joshua's lovemaking. Until this moment she had not realised quite how much she had missed it.

'I'm glad you like it.' In an effort to conceal the

turmoil within her her voice was as low as she could make it.

'It's not the only thing I like. I think I can say the same for you.'

Fingers that had been on her throat now slid beneath the fabric of her blouse, trailing an erotic path along skin that was as sensitive as if the nerve-ends had been exposed.

A trembling took Jenny, but within seconds she had it under control. But its violence, coupled with the expression in the grey eyes that held hers in the mirror, told her that Joshua had felt it.

'What do you mean?' she whispered.

For answer he bent over her, his hands moving down her back, moulding themselves to her waist and her hips, then curving up to cup her breasts. The movement brought her head slightly back, and his own head came easily to meet it, his mouth just inches from hers.

'This is what I mean,' he said, his breath mingling with hers.

Her lips parted almost of their own volition. She let herself shape against him, fitting against the lines of his body as if so designed. He seemed to be all about her; the hardness of his long length against her back, his head bending over her to the front. There was no thought as she responded to his kiss. Her hands lifted and groped for his hair, and the blood was singing in her veins. As he began to explore the sweetness of her mouth she knew that she had been waiting for this moment.

Presently he lifted his head to draw breath.

'Stand up,' he muttered, turning her and drawing her up. She came to him willingly, letting him weld her against him.

'Say it,' he commanded, and she heard the huskiness in his tone.

'Say what?'

'That you like it.' His mouth was so close to hers that she could feel his lips moving against hers as he talked.

'I like it, you rascal!'

His teeth nibbled softly on the trembling lips, sending fresh fires coursing through her. Then he asked, 'Why the hell have you been avoiding me?' He drew back his head and looked down at her. 'You don't really care about that idiot Bruce, do you?'

How could she care about Bruce? It was not possible to be in love with two men at the same time. At the silent thought she froze. Till this moment she had never admitted consciously to herself that she loved Joshua.

'Say it, Jenny. Bruce never made love to you the way I do.'

Violet eyes were troubled as she looked at him. That was all it meant to Joshua—a physical thing. There was no question of the chemistry between them, or that he wanted her as much as she wanted him. But for Joshua the wanting extended only to the fulfilment of a physical need. For Jenny herself the need was all-encompassing; physical, to be sure, but spiritual also. She knew now that she loved Joshua, and loving entailed companionship and affection and growing old together just as much as it entailed the magic of two rapturous bodies.

'Jenny!'

'It's true,' she said unsteadily. 'He never did.'

'And you never slept with him?'

She met the gaze of the dark grey eyes. 'I've never slept with anybody.'

'You're going to sleep with me.' His voice was gentle now, but firm. The words were a statement, not a question. 'You know that, Jenny, don't you?'

If her mind didn't know it by now, her body certainly did. There was a wild clamouring of her senses, a need such as she had never experienced. Jenny knew that if Joshua pressed her to surrender totally, she was no longer strong enough to put up any defence against him. Her heart told her she did not want to put up any defence; that she should allow him to carry her to the bed. Only some last vestige of rational thinking warned her to put a stop to his lovemaking while she still could.

His fingers were on her blouse, opening the buttons. It was all she could do not to let her own hands go beneath his shirt, to plant themselves against the muscled chest.

With the strength of a baby she pushed against him. 'Someone will see us!'

'We'll lock the door.'

'Anna knows where I am.' And as he drew her to him, 'It's the middle of the morning, for heaven's sake! Anyone might come looking for me.'

Joshua went on holding her a moment longer. She heard him laugh, that deep seductive sound which at the best of times was unnerving. 'You're a coward, Jenny Malloy,' he muttered, releasing her. 'You're off the hook for now. But next time I won't stop.'

He was walking towards the door when he stopped. 'You turned me on and I forgot what I came here to say.'

'That you were satisfied with the rondavels,' she managed.

'Ah, yes. The rest follows from there. We have a visitor arriving on Friday.'

She looked at him searchingly. The few seconds had allowed her to regain some measure of composure. 'Someone new? Not one of the regulars?'

'She's flying here from the States.'

An icy hand gripped Jenny's heart. 'A . . . a friend of yours?'

'Maybelle is a friend, yes. I'm keen that Impalavlei makes a good impression.'

'We can only do our best,' Jenny said tonelessly.

Joshua left the rondavel. She watched him walk past the window and down the path that led to the main building, a tall figure, lithe and strong and supremely sure of himself. His walk was loose and supple, and he was whistling as if nothing of importance had happened.

Joshua had enjoyed their lovemaking, Jenny thought, but it had ceased to exist for him the moment that it had ended. Even now his thoughts were somewhere else. On his next project, perhaps. Or on Maybelle, the friend who was flying all the way from America to South Africa just to spend a few days at Impalavlei.

Feeling more than a little ill, Jenny returned to the dressing-table and sat down. As she looked up her gaze hit the mirror. Was that really Jenny Malloy, that image that stared back at her? A girl with lips that were soft and kiss-bruised; with cheeks that were too red; with eyes that were wild and distraught: with hair that looked as if it had not seen a brush in days?

Her blouse was still open—she had forgotten that Joshua had undone the buttons—and as she sat forward she saw the curves and shadows of her breasts. Again she felt as if she was seeing something different. For surely that was a new voluptuousness that met her eyes, a female ripeness that she had not possessed before.

Angrily she blinked her eyes and did up the blouse. Then she went to the bathroom and splashed cold water on to her face. Somehow she had to restore some order to her appearance before she ventured back into the gounds of the camp.

If only she could restore order to her frenzied senses! A little more persuasion and she would have surrendered to Joshua. And afterwards the sense of anti-climax would have been even greater than it was now. For she would have given up more than her virginity; loving him as she did she would have given him the very essence of herself.

To learn about Maybelle just a moment later would have destroyed her. Jenny knew that just as surely as if it had actually happened.

CHAPTER EIGHT

JOSHUA drove to the station himself to meet Maybelle Hunter. When the car returned and Jenny saw a tall willowy blonde uncoil herself from the passenger's seat she knew that her worst fears had materialised, for Maybelle was beautiful.

Even after hours of driving her appearance was immaculate. Blonde hair fell to her shoulders in smooth shining ripples. Eyes, set in a creamy skin, were deep blue and a smile revealed teeth that were as flawless as any film star's.

Tucking a hand through Joshua's arm, she looked around her, and Jenny heard her say, 'Darling, it's magnificent! The atmosphere is gorgeous—so basic and primitive.'

Her voice was low and husky. She would have a sexy voice, Jenny thought with a touch of envy. Everything about Maybelle was perfect. No wonder Joshua had wanted the setting to be just right too!

'Jenny,' Joshua called, 'come and meet Maybelle.'

Blue eyes sized her up, assessingly, Jenny thought. Then Maybelle stretched out a hand and said, 'I'm so glad to meet you, Jenny. Joshua has been telling me about you.'

'Only good, I hope.' Jenny mouthed the cliché,

then couldn't help adding, 'I'm surprised he found the time, Miss Hunter.'

There was a second of silence. Jenny did not look at Joshua. She did not need to in order to know that he would have registered the double snub.

Maybelle covered the silence by saying, 'I do hope I've brought the right clothes.' She gestured down at her superbly-tailored safari-style slack-suit. 'What do you think? Is it simple enough?'

'It's nice and basic.' Jenny smiled politely. 'Did you buy it in Fifth Avenue, New York?'

This time Maybelle made no attempt to cover the silence. Well-outlined lips still framed the perfect teeth in a smile, but the blue eyes had become decidedly frosty, as if she had recognised an adversary where she had least expected to find one.

Involuntarily Jenny glanced at Joshua. His lips had thinned, his expression was furious. That he made no comment, she realised, was only due to Maybelle's presence. He looked as if he would have liked to shake Jenny till her teeth rattled.

Coupled with a thrill of alarm, Jenny was conscious of intense satisfaction. Her eyes sparkled as she said, 'You must be thirsty after the long trip, Miss Hunter. If you'll excuse me I'll organise sandwiches and a cool drink.' A glance sideways. 'I'm sure Joshua will show you to your rondavel.'

Maybelle's rondavel was the one next to Joshua's—at his own request. Jenny knew every detail of the furnishings. The rondavel was her favourite—or had been until now.

Lunchtime came and went. Maybelle would have no food of her own, she would be eating with Joshua. Jenny did not see either of them; they would be together in his rondavel, she assumed. She told herself she did not care, and pushed away the thought of an intimacy from which she was excluded.

A little later she saw the Land Rover drive out of the camp gate. Joshua was driving, and beside him was a blonde head. No use telling herself that she did not care, Jenny knew, as she watched the vehicle vanish from sight. She cared so much that she would have liked to kill them both.

She remembered Joshua's first day at Impalavlei, when she had driven him about the park. Now he was driving Maybelle. Somewhere in the situation there seemed a conflict of loyalties, particularly after what had so recently passed between Joshua and herself. Angrily she dashed a tear from her cheeks, and wished she could as easily remove the feeling of betrayal.

It was almost dark when the Land Rover returned. Anna appeared with an invitation from Joshua, asking Jenny to join Maybelle and himself in a braaivleis supper. Part of her wanted to accept, but she sent back word that she was tired and planned an early night.

She did in fact have a headache. Normally she would have walked a while by the camp fence, enjoying the coolness that came with the evening, but tonight she chose not to. It was almost inevitable that she would walk into Joshua and Maybelle. Perhaps she would even see them kissing. Just the thought of such a scene was enough to evoke pain. The sight itself would be more than she could endure.

For a while she tried to read, but she gave up the effort when she realised that she was unable to take in a word. There was nothing to do but go to bed. It was very hot in the room. Slipping naked between the cool sheets gave a few minutes of relief.

She was half asleep when the door opened. She jerked in alarm, clutching the sheet beneath her chin, and wondered how she could have been so trusting as to leave the door open.

Joshua! Even had she not been able to make out the lithe tallness of his silhouette she would have known it was him. Making her breathing as slow as she was able—no mean feat when she was as wound up as a frightened kitten—she lay still.

In two strides he was beside her bed. Jenny had never been more conscious of the aura he seemed to carry with him at all times; the air in the room crackled with it.

She opened her eyes a mere slit. There was just enough light in the room to make out his outline. She did not see his face, she did not need to, she could picture his expression merely by the impression of angry tautness in his bearing. He looked as powerful and as dangerous as a jungle animal. The breath jerked in her lungs so that it was an effort to maintain the slow breathing.

'Call off the act, Jenny.' She had never heard

his voice quite so harsh. 'You're not asleep.'

A few seconds of silence. He was looking down at her, Jenny knew. Her own eyes were tightly closed now. She could not remember a time when she had felt quite so tense.

When she felt her shoulders gripped and pulled upwards she was not surprised. From the moment Joshua had entered her room she had expected something of the sort. Nevertheless, the roughness of the movement and the tension that accompanied it made her gasp.

Forgetting her charade, she slapped him hard across the cheek. The sound was a staccato shot in the stillness.

She heard his swift intake of breath. Then he said harshly, 'So you like to play rough, Jenny Malloy. The sweet exterior is just for show.'

'Get out!' she hissed.

'That's not what you want.' His tone was laced with contempt. 'This is.'

Another swift movement as he tore the sheet from her clutching hand. He stood quite still a moment looking down at her. Though she could not see his eyes, she saw the mocking curve of the lips.

'I should have known,' he drawled. 'The unlocked door—now this. If it was sex you wanted, why didn't you say so?'

She had never been so angry. At that moment she hated him. Through the wild clamouring of her body, she still hated him.

'I always sleep with an unlocked door,' she said through clenched teeth. 'Nobody at Impalavlei was ever thought to abuse the situation. I'll know better now.'

'Do you always sleep in the nude?' he drawled.

'When I'm hot.'

'Like now.' His tone had become lazy, outrageous. There was no mistaking his meaning. 'You're a hotblooded female, little Jenny. The other day, in the rondavel, you wanted to sleep with me—don't waste your breath denying it. What made you change your mind? Were you playing hard to get?'

'You're a swine, Joshua Adams!' Her voice was choked with bitterness.

'For stating the truth?' Without warning he pushed her back against the sheet, and then she felt his tongue in the hollow between her breasts; moving slowly upwards, tracing the path of the gentle swell.

Jenny lay rigid as her body quickened in a familiar response. Her hands clenched themselves into tight fists. She would *not* bury her fingers in his hair even though every nerve and fibre of her body wanted her to do just that. There was nothing she could do about the hardening response of her breasts—a response which Joshua would have registered with satisfaction—but that was all the reaction he would get from her.

'You were waiting for me.' Joshua had lifted his head and was looking down at her.

'That's not true,' she got out. She felt so dizzy that she hardly knew what she said. 'You and Maybelle, in your rondavel . . . I thought you were . . .'

She stopped then, but too late. She felt his hand go to her throat, his fingers resting very lightly on the frenzied pulse. 'So you're jealous of Maybelle.'

Violently she shook her head. 'I don't give a damn about her! Or about you for that matter!'

'Is that why you were so rude to her this morning?' His voice was soft, dangerous.

His hands had left her now. Taking her chance, Jenny snatched the sheet back to her chin, but with an easy movement Joshua yanked the sheet down again.

'Well, Jenny?'

'I was polite,' she managed.

'Like hell you were! You were a frigid little bitch! And that after I told you how anxious I was that Impalavlei make a good impression on Maybelle.'

The pain that had been with her ever since she had learned of Maybelle's existence grew stronger. 'Just leave me, Joshua. What Maybelle thinks of Impalavlei doesn't matter to me.'

'It had better worry you,' he said roughly. 'Maybelle is a tour guide with a big agency. If she decides to make Impalavlei a base it would go a long way to putting us on our feet.'

She looked at him through a daze. 'That's why she came . . .? Why you took her driving? Joshua, you said she was a friend . . .'

'She is.' An enigmatic quality in his tone. 'Are you jealous, Jenny?'

Oh yes, she was jealous. All day she had been jealous. But there was something she needed to understand. Ignoring a question that needed no answer, she said, 'All the improvements . . . were they all for Maybelle's benefit?'

'You know the answer to that.' His voice was hard.

'I never should have stopped fighting you,' Jenny burst out.

'You haven't stopped. Today . . .' his words trailed away as he pulled her roughly to him and covered her mouth with his own. His kiss was hard and brutal; punishing, as if he was venting an anger he had no other way of expressing, but Jenny kept her mouth tightly closed against him as she tried to twist her head away.

This was not how their lovemaking should be. Through her anger she remembered the last time, in the renovated rondavel; the way her body had responded to his and how near she had been to a total surrender. Then there had been a magic in the closeness of their bodies. Now there was only brute force on his side and outrage on hers. If he were to plead with her she would not give in to him.

And yet through the anger of her mind, she could feel a familiar quickening of her senses. Against the bareness of her breasts there was the feel of Joshua's wool sweater, and beyond that the fierce beat of his heart. In her nostrils was the composite smell of maleness that she would always associate with Joshua, even after he had disappeared from her life. In her legs was an aching weakness. Once again, Jenny knew, her body was betraying her against the dictates of her mind.

Somehow she managed to insert her fists between her chest and his, and taking advantage of a moment when he lifted his head for breath, she pushed hard against him. 'I'll scream if you don't go!' she hissed through clenched teeth.

'I was just going.' He released her abruptly, so suddenly that she fell back hard against the bed. He stood beside it, a tall threatening figure, his breathing just a little ragged. 'I warn you, Jenny, behave yourself—at least while Maybelle is here. If you don't, I promise that you'll suffer for it.'

He did not wait for an answer. Without a word of goodnight he strode out of the room.

When Jenny had locked the door, she went back to bed. And then, realising that she would not sleep, she slipped on jeans and a warm angora sweater and went outside.

The camp was hushed and peaceful. Save for a light in Joshua's rondavel, the compound was in darkness. Was Joshua alone, or was he with Maybelle once more? If the answer were the latter, she did not want to know it, Jenny thought, as she tried to erase the inevitable picture from her mind. Even now, hating Joshua as she did tonight, the picture brought a searing pain.

Alone in the whispering darkness, Jenny posed questions to herself, and found a few answers. As her feelings for Joshua had grown, so her opposition to his wishes had waned. Perhaps that was what loving a person did to one, she reflected unhappily. She had already experienced the betrayal of her own senses. Perhaps falling in love could also lead to a twisting of one's convictions.

It had taken a while before she had acknowledged to herself that she loved Joshua, but even before that she had fought him less than at the start.

She had wanted to believe him, had wanted to believe that he had the interests of Impalavlei at heart. That he did in fact regard it was the home he had left so long ago, that it was not just an investment whose value and productivity had needed to be enhanced.

Her present anger had not affected the understanding that Joshua's changes had in fact been for the good. It was his motives which had shattered her illusions. She no longer believed that his concern had stemmed from an affection for Impalavlei—the bushveld and its animals. She knew now that all along his sole interest in the game park had been from an investment point of view. When he had said that he had regarded Impalavlei as home he had been trying to win her over, nothing else. It had been easier to work with Jenny as a friend, rather than as an enemy.

A hyena's laugh rent the stillness. The sound was eerie; laughter that seemed to speak more of anger and distress than amusement. In Jenny's unhappiness she saw it as an echo of her own feelings. It was time to come to terms with the situation.

She recalled Joshua's first day, and her hope that he would not stay long at Impalavlei; the premonition that if he did it could mean disaster for her own peace of mind. She wondered now if there had been an actual moment when she had fallen in love with Joshua—wondered too if she could have prevented it. For all along it had been clear that such a love would hold no future.

In the starlit darkness the stone wall was an opaque shape. Without thinking, Jenny had walked towards it, her refuge for meditation, the place where she could give her emotions free rein. She leaned against it.

She knew now that loving Joshua as she did, she had endowed him with an idealism he did not possess. And though she had tried not to, she had also allowed herself to think of a life which could not exist. Telling herself there could be no future with him was one thing; dreaming of being with him always was another.

With Maybelle's coming, Jenny had been forced to recognise her own foolishness. A tour guide, Joshua had called her. Perhaps she was that. In addition she was the woman in his life—everything pointed to it. There had been Joshua's anxiety that Impalavlei present its best image for Maybelle's arrival. There had been the proprietorial hand on his arm, the husky-voiced 'Darling'.

There had been the drive through the game park during which Jenny had endured the pangs of a jealousy she had never known before. Seeing Bruce with a girl in the night-club in Pretoria had produced no such feelings of jealousy. There had been only a feeling of anger that her fiancé had not been honest with her. The jealousy Jenny had felt today was a new emotion, and while she despised it, she knew that it came from loving foolishly and too intensely.

She wondered how long Maybelle would

remain at Impalavlei. A few days, Joshua had said, when Jenny had questioned him. With luck the stay would not last more than a week—and even that would be too long. She wondered how she would endure seeing them together all the time.

Eventually Maybelle would go back to America, and if she had liked what she had seen at Impalavlei she would arrange for tours to the game park. But Maybelle herself would be back long before the tours became reality. Jenny had only to think of her emotions to understand how the other girl felt about Joshua. Fortunately for Maybelle, it appeared that her feelings were reciprocated. Joshua would await her return as eagerly as he had anticipated her arrival today.

Would they be married? Or would Maybelle merely make Impalavlei a semi-permanent base for herself, content to live with Joshua whenever she could? Either way, Jenny knew she could not tolerate the situation. She knew it as definitely as she had ever known anything in her life. Watching Maybelle and Joshua together for just a few hours had been painful. Being with them day in and day out in the limited confines of the camp, witnessing an intimacy from which she must inevitably be excluded, would be totally unbearable.

She herself must leave Impalavlei; the decision seemed to come of itself. A Girl Friday could perform the duties she did now. Joshua would not know the difference.

Was this what it had all come to? she wondered. On another night, at this same spot, she had resolved to remain here, had made a silent promise to fight for what she had considered right, to protect the sanctuary which had been her father's life.

Just a few weeks later, she was about to go back on that promise. She thought of her father. The picture that came to her was of an elderly man standing by the fence, gazing across the river into the throbbing veld with the look of one who never grew tired of his surroundings. The stem of a pipe would be between his teeth, and the expression in faded eyes would be one of serene kindness.

Kindness. The quality had been her father's hallmark. Kindness towards animals and towards people. Kindness towards the daughter whom he had loved. With a sudden lifting of the heart Jenny knew that because of this kindness her father would have understood her need to get away. He would not have seen it as betrayal. Rather he would have acknowledged her decision as the sensible path to preserving her sanity.

Tomorrow she would take the first step along that path. She would draft an advertisement, and George would take it with him the next time he went to post letters in the box some distance beyond the park gates. When Maybelle had gone Jenny would tell Joshua her decision.

She kept her shoulders high as she went on walking through the fragrant darkness. She had found a way of coping with her problem; that in itself should be a source of satisfaction. Yet as she put her hand to the door and entered the silent room, she felt unutterably sad.

Maybelle remained at Impalavlei a little more than a week, and to Jenny the time seemed more like months. The air of familiarity she had glimpsed the first day never vanished. Maybelle was constantly touching Joshua. The possessive hand on his arm had become a familiar sight. Often she put a hand on his waist, an outwardly playful gesture which, Jenny knew, was anything but playful. The blonde hair—always smooth, never dishevelled—swung in a golden curtain when she leaned her head back to laugh at him. The husky voice seemed to become a part of the very air. There were times when Jenny heard it in her sleep.

To Jenny, Maybelle's manner was an irritant. Her laugh seemed unnaturally sensual, as if she was putting it on solely for Joshua's benefit. Her vivaciousness did not pall; Jenny wondered if Maybelle ever experienced low moods. The possessive touch bespoke an intimacy which provoked pain in her each time she saw it.

But if Jenny was disturbed by Maybelle's manner, Joshua appeared fascinated. The glossy dark head would incline courteously when the other girl spoke, and his laugh rang out often in response to hers. When she put her hand on his waist, his arm would go around her shoulders. Clearly Maybelle was making no presumptions. Joshua's interest matched her own.

Towards Jenny Maybelle maintained a somewhat cool friendliness. Now and then the blue eyes would rest assessingly on the tumbled dark hair, and the perfectly-painted lips would tighten just a little. Was she imagining Jenny and Joshua alone at the game park? Jenny wondered. Did the thought cause her even the slightest pain? For if it did, there was no reason for it. It was true that Joshua had made love to her more thoroughly than any man had done before. But it had meant nothing to him on an emotional level. A woman as worldly as Maybelle would understand that Joshua was a red-blooded male with a need to enjoy himself. It had been nothing more to him than that. Maybelle's claim was secure.

Generally contact between the two girls was limited. Maybelle displayed much interest in Impalavlei. She wanted to know about accommodation and other facilities, and was intrigued with the tree-tops viewing platform under construction some way out of the camp. Now and then she directed her questions to Jenny, but her manner then was remote and matter-of-fact. Jenny did not repeat her rudeness of the first day, but she felt sure that Maybelle had not forgotten it. The rapport between the two girls was minimal. In the main Maybelle's contact was with Joshua.

A week had never seemed so long. Jenny breathed a long sigh of relief when Joshua loaded the expensive luggage into the Land Rover. 'Be seeing you next time I come,' said Maybelle as she made ready to leave.

Jenny managed a smile. 'That will be very nice. Have a good trip back.'

The smile vanished as the Land Rover left the camp gates and took to the road. Maybelle would not be seeing her on her next visit. Long before then Jenny would have returned to Pretoria.

The advertisement for a Girl Friday would have had its first publication in yesterday's newspapers. Soon now replies would begin to arrive in the mail. She would wait for a suitable applicant, Jenny resolved, then she would make arrangements to leave.

Thus far Joshua knew nothing of her plans. Until there was something definite to tell him, she would keep her silence.

Jenny was seated at her desk, a ledger open in front of her. A slight frown creased her forehead as she worked. In just a short time the finances of Impalavlei had improved. A look at the reservations for the next month showed that accommodation figures were improving. Somehow word of the improvements had begun to spread.

'Jenny!'

A long shadow had formed on the sunlit floor beside the desk. She looked up and felt her heart miss a beat. It was one thing to despise Joshua for his motives; quite another to remain immune to his appeal. From her vantage point on the stool, he looked even taller than usual. His tan was emphasised by the rust shade of his shirt, and where it was unbuttoned she caught a glimpse of bare chest. A slight quiver shuddered through her as she experienced a sharp longing to lean her cheek against it. The gaunt face had a look of freshness, and in his eyes was a warmth which she saw in her dreams every night.

She swallowed. 'Did you want something, Joshua?'

'I'm taking you for a drive.'

She kept her face carefully expressionless to hide her sudden excitement at being alone with him. 'I . . . I'm working.'

A tanned hand reached across the desk and closed the ledger. 'Come along, poppet.'

It seemed an age since he had used the endearment. Not since their lovemaking in the rondavel, after which he had sprung the news of Maybelle's coming, had there been any warmth or easiness between them. The wise thing would be to refuse him, but it was hard to say the words when her senses protested against them.

Joshua resolved her conflict by drawing her to her feet. 'You haven't seen the viewing platform,' he told her. The grip on her wrist was firm.

She could have resisted him, she knew, as she sat beside him in the Land Rover just a few minutes later. But there were times when common sense took second place to the dictates of her heart. Very soon now she would be gone from Impalavlei and she might never see Joshua again. By going with him now she might have one more memory to cherish in the years ahead.

A memory to add to all the others. Always in her mind there would be a picture of Joshua at sunset, the planes of his face made mellow by the fading light: the meals they had shared by the tree with the kerosene lamp hanging from it; the evening in Pretoria, and the ardour of their lovemaking.

Memories that would bring pain, but with it a kind of consolation too. For they would remind her of the man she loved more than she had ever thought possible. Even after she had understood that Joshua's ideas were in utter contradiction to her own, and that all his improvements had in fact been made with the sole purpose of enhancing the financial value of Impalavlei, that love had not waned. A little despairingly she knew that she would probably love him always.

A flash of black and white caught her attention. Joshua had seen it too, for the car draw to a halt. Some yards from the road a herd of zebra grazed. Their bodies were sleek and powerful, the stripes a dramatic pattern against the dun-coloured bush. The proud heads turned in the direction of the car, and then, of one accord, they galloped from sight.

'They've returned,' Jenny said softly, turning to Joshua. Her eyes were shining. It was a long while since such a herd had roamed Impalavlei.

An enigmatic gaze rested on the small flushed face, noting the radiant smile, lingering on luminous eyes, on lips that were parted to reveal small even teeth, moving to the slender throat and the swell of breasts just visible beneath the snug-fitting T-shirt.

'Others will return too.' He spoke with quiet satisfaction. 'Did you miss the dust, poppet?'

She knew what he meant. Zebra were shy animals. Even now they had run off just seconds after the car had come to a stop. Had there been a cloud of dust the herd might have been out of sight before the dust had had time to subside. It came to her that the tarred roads were not an intrusion in the wildness of the terrain.

'You were right to pave,' she said quietly, then turned away as the car started once more.

Joshua had been right in so many of the things he had planned, she realised, not for the first time. The bringing of water had indeed seen the return of much of the game. Only yesterday a guest had returned to camp in excitement after spotting a family of lions.

The rondavels and the lounge and the office were bright and inviting while blending with the atmosphere of the camp. The restaurant had not yet been completed, but Jenny had seen enough of it to know that its presence would do nothing to jar the feeling of rustic serenity. The picture window in the lounge had been an inspired addition. When the chill of evening was in the air, and when the light was too dim to allow for travel on the roads, guests could sit by the window and gaze across the river and into the darkening bush.

She had to acknowledge that Joshua's plans had been skilfully conceived and carried out. Only his motives were suspect.

Lost in thought, she was puzzled when she felt the car slow to a halt once more. If there was any game she had not seen it. She turned to Joshua, a question in her eyes, and saw him gesture.

A little way ahead was a clump of mopani trees. The day was windless, the veld still. Only the branches of one tree showed sign of movement, a curved grey outline just visible above them.

'Elephant!' Jenny breathed.

The car inched forward again, very slowly this time. When it drew to a halt once more, the engine was left running. It seemed Joshua knew the importance of a quick getaway in the remote event that an elephant might decide to charge.

Now the animal was in better view. Long tusks gleamed whitely against the dark foliage, and the parchment-like ears flapped in the movement which had alerted Joshua's attention to the animal's presence. Its trunk was curled around the tree, and as Jenny and Joshua watched, fascinated, the tree was bent as easily as if it had been a brittle twig.

Releasing the tree, the elephant turned its eyes towards the car. The trunk lifted, and a low trumpeting sound rolled across the silent land. Jenny watched raptly. She had seen many elephants in her life, but the sight never failed to thrill her. This time the sight was especially poignant, for she knew from George, the old tracker, just how long it had been since there had been elephants at Impalavlei.

Almost without thinking she found herself looking at Joshua. As always, she was stirred by the strength in the ascetic profile, the sense of purpose in the firm line of his jaw. As if he sensed himself being watched, he turned in his seat. The dark eyes held a sparkle and his lips were curved in a smile.

No need to ask him if he was satisfied with the ever-increasing return of the bigger game, Jenny realised. His expression spoke for itself. Never before had so many guests been expected at Impalavlei. They would not leave the game park disappointed.

The elephant played with the tree a few minutes longer, then it turned and lumbered into the bush, and Joshua drove slowly onward.

Jenny wondered if he was waiting for her to make a comment. He would not know that at that moment she was incapable of speech. She was trembling as she glued unfocused eyes to the window. It was all she could do to stop the trembling from becoming visible.

She had not yet told Joshua that there was an applicant for the post of Girl Friday. The letter had arrived in yesterday's mail, and the applicant seemed to meet all the necessary requirements. Jenny had replied to her this morning, asking her to come for an interview, and George had gone to post the letter.

There was no valid reason why she had withheld the news from Joshua, no reason why she quailed at the thought of telling him. For Joshua would not miss her. If anything he would find it easier to work with someone who did not oppose him. She would tell him today, she decided. She could keep the secret no longer.

Blinking away the tears that had gathered in her eyes, Jenny tried to concentrate on the passing scenery. If only there was a way of memorising every tree, every bush, every animal! For she knew already that while Joshua was at Impalavlei she would not come back, not even for a holiday.

There was no need to memorise Joshua's face.

Every chiselled feature was etched in her mind with a sharpness that would not fade as long as she lived.

The tree in which Joshua had chosen to build the viewing platform was enormous. It was also very beautiful. It stood just a small way distant from a bend in the river. On the near side was a sandy bank marked with the prints of many animals, and the eye of experience told Jenny that many of the prints were fresh. Joshua had indeed chosen well.

It was the first time Jenny had been here. Pride had taken precedence over curiosity, so that she had not wanted to give Joshua the pleasure of inspecting the innovation that seemed to mean a great deal to him.

There was still some work to be done on the platform, but today was Saturday, and the place was deserted. Staring upwards, Jenny guessed that the platform would become one of Impalavlei's most popular features. It would be a spot where people could observe the animals from a height that made vision easier; where photographers would be able to sit for hours in comfort.

'Well, Jenny?' His voice, vital and alive, brought her swinging round.

'It's very nice,' she offered.

Something flickered in his eyes. 'A mild comment, coming from you, Jenny.'

He would not have expected the rapturous enthusiasm he no doubt had received from Maybelle. Perhaps what he had expected from Jenny was a withering scorn. He could not know that the fight seemed to have gone out of her. With her departure from Impalavlei so imminent, what had once been of great meaning was so no longer. Nor would he be able to guess that her greatest unhappiness lay in the knowledge that she would never see him again. That, she resolved fiercely, was something he would never know.

'Can we go up?' she asked, less because she wanted to examine the platform than to lessen a mood.

'That's the idea. Come along, Jenny.'

For some distance around the tree the bushes had been cleared. A person walking the few feet from his car to the ladder that reached to the platform would not be surprised by hidden predators.

As she climbed the ladder, Jenny was acutely aware of the lithe body close behind her. It was so long since they had been alone together; too long, said her demanding senses.

She was knifed by a sharp stab of need. She wanted to feel his arms around her once more, his lips exploring her mouth. Appalled, she tried to thrust the longing from her. To submit to his lovemaking, assuming he was so inclined, would be only to store up more eventual unhappiness.

She would tell Joshua of her decision to leave Impalavlei. She would tell him just as soon as they reached the platform. Intuitively she knew that the sooner she got the telling over the better.

He gave her no chance to talk. He was eager to

show her the platform. To explain what still remained to be done. To discuss the furnishings—they would put in just the basics, he said.

The view across the river and on to the sandy banks was even more impressive than Jenny had imagined. Even more than before, she knew that the platform would prove an attraction to tourists, knew too that it was not in bad taste. As with everything else he had planned, Joshua had seen to it that the viewing platform blended with the surroundings.

Eventually it would be enclosed with glass, Jenny supposed. Now there was only a wooden hand-rail that went around the wooden-boarded floor. Jenny stood at the rail and looked over the bush. It was time to speak. And then Joshua came to stand next to her. She could feel the length of an arm brush against hers, and the need that had been in her grew so strong that it was only with an effort of will that she managed to stop herself from turning and putting her face against his chest.

Surely he must feel the vibrations that sparked between them, she thought wildly. She was so near to him that it was not possible that he did not feel the burning warmth of her body, or the slight trembling that she was unable to contain. Move away from me, Joshua, she pleaded silently, because I'm too weak to move away myself.

His exclamation rang out suddenly, and she jerked round, caught by his vehemence. His eyes were on a point some way beyond the platform, and following the direction of his gaze, Jenny saw a single impala.

It took a moment for her to realise that the animal was in trouble. One fragile leg appeared to be trapped beside a pile of building materials. Vainly it struggled to get free.

There was something desperate about its movements. The graceful head turned frantically this way and that, at the same time the little body pulled so hard that it seemed as if the leg would snap.

'Lion!'

Jenny froze at the one word. Some distance away in the bushes was a flash of tawny brown. She turned back to Joshua, and saw that his face was set and hard. Beneath the tan the corners of his nostrils seemed to have whitened. In one stride he was at the top of the ladder.

'Joshua!' A wild scream. And when he did not respond, she was running to him, pulling at his arm. He was already on the ladder.

'No, Jenny!' He jerked himself free.

'You'll get killed!'

For just one moment the grey eyes searched her face, in them an expression she knew that she would always remember. 'I'll be fine,' he said, as he moved rapidly downward.

CHAPTER NINE

THERE was no stopping him. As she watched him go she knew she had never been more frightened. 'Joshua, I love you!' She called the words after him, but he did not hear them, for her throat was so constricted that her voice came out in a choked whisper.

And then it was back to the wooden rail. On the ground Joshua was moving with lightning speed. In a second he had reached the impala, was freeing it from its deathly trap. He was back at the ladder, the small animal in his arms, as the lion emerged from the bush. As easily as if the animal was no heavier than a kitten, he skimmed up the wooden rungs. It was then that the first enraged roar rent the air.

'Joshua! Oh God, you're safe!' Jenny ran to the edge of the ladder.

'Help me.' He thrust the animal towards her.

She took it from him, held the shivering body, all awkward lines and unused to human hands, as Joshua joined her on the ladder.

'You're safe,' she said again, and did not know that she was crying.

'Jenny.' Her name had never been said so gently, as he took the impala from her and put it down on the wooden floor.

Then he turned back to her. She was moving into his arms at the same time as he was drawing her into them. For a moment that seemed to have no meaning in time he held her against him. In her throat and in her chest she could feel the wild beating of her pulses, a product of the fear she had experienced. Against her she could feel the beating of his own heart, strong and quickened as well. There was no thought as she pressed her mouth against the bare skin of his chest where his buttons were open. When she felt his lips in her hair there was just the wonderful comfort of knowing that he was alive.

And then he had released her and had gone to the shivering animal. He bent, stroking the impala to soothe its fright, before taking the injured leg gently in his hand.

'Why did you do it?' Jenny asked.

'I had to.'

'The law of the jungle.' Jenny searched for words. 'You . . . there's no way you could help every animal about to be hunted.'

'I wouldn't try.' He looked up from his squatting position and she saw the anger in his eyes. 'This had nothing to do with the jungle, with nature. It was carelessness—man's carelessness. A wire where it had no place to be.'

Jenny bit her lip. 'You put yourself in terrible danger.'

'There was no choice.'

She watched as he took the water bottle from his belt and poured a few drops over the wound.

The little wild creature was still shivering, but it was not struggling to free itself from Joshua's hands. It was as if it trusted this big man with the strong hands and the unexpected gentleness in his touch.

As she herself trusted him, Jenny thought as she squatted beside him, helping him where she could. She had misjudged Joshua. She knew it now when it was too late. She had never let herself believe that he cared for Impalavlei and its animals; had been convinced that all he did was for the wrong motives.

But he did care after all. The life of one small animal meant little in the general scheme of things. Yet Joshua must care very much to have rescued the impala when by doing so he had placed his own life at stake.

She had behaved foolishly all along. Though there could be no future with Joshua—soon Maybelle would join him again—she could have enjoyed the time she had spent with him. Loving him as much as she did, there would have been days of harmony to look back on. As it was, he must have regarded her as childish in the extreme.

For a few minutes they worked together without speaking. Joshua bathed and dressed the wound, while Jenny held the leg and stroked the little animal. From below came the angry roars of the thwarted lion. This too she would remember, Jenny thought.

'What will we do with the impala?' she asked when Joshua had tied his handkerchief firmly around the animal's leg.

'Take it back to camp. In a few days, when the wound has healed, we'll let it go.'

There had been a special atmosphere between them for a few minutes. Speech had cut into it. Jenny went to the wooden railing. So absorbed had she been with the impala that while she had heard the lion's roars she had not considered the implications.

Looking down, she went rigid. Pacing the ground between the ladder and the Land Rover was the lion, a male lion with a black mane and a mangy-looking coat. Jenny watched in frozen horror as it threw its mouth wide and let out another bloodcurdling roar.

She turned as Joshua joined her at the railing. His mouth was set, but in his eyes sparked a daredevil light. It came to Jenny that Joshua was not frightened by the narrowness of his escape. He was stimulated by the sense of danger and adventure. As she herself felt stimulated, Jenny realised after a moment.

'What now?' she asked.

'Not much we can do.' He shrugged. 'Leo feels cheated. He knows the impala is here and he wants it.' He paused thoughtfully. 'He looks old, Jenny. Perhaps he's been wounded himself and has trouble hunting. The impala would have been an easy prey.'

There was no way they could cross the small patch of ground between the ladder and the Land Rover while the lion paced there. He was as enraged a lion as Jenny had ever seen. Not only would he attack the impala, he might savage Joshua and herself as well.

'He could stay here for hours,' she observed.

'Then we'll have to stay too.'

Caught by the inflection in Joshua's tone, she jerked up her head once more to look at him, and an odd tremor ran through her. The lion could remain here for hours, Joshua had said. She knew he was right. But soon night would fall. She looked around the small exposed platform. She could not, would not, remain alone here with Joshua.

'We can't stay.' She did not know that her eyes were wide and troubled; did not know that to the watching man she looked like a small ruffled elf who had come face to face with a fact that was unpalatable.

'We've no option.' His teeth flashed in a wicked grin. 'Might as well make yourself comfortable, poppet. Could be a long wait.'

Time passed. The impala now lay quietly on the wooden floor. It was a tribute to Joshua and herself, Jenny thought, that it felt secure enough to do so.

The two humans squatted not far from it. There was an unimpeded view to the river. On the near side nothing moved. No animal would dare to drink so near to the hungry lion. On the far side, however, where the bank sloped away from the bush, animals appeared. This was the river which flowed past the camp; one of the few which held water even in the dry season.

Once two giraffe came through the trees.

Unperturbed by the lion's roars, they stopped at the edge of the bank, spread their legs wide and bent their long necks towards the water. It was an ungainly sight, and yet strangely graceful too, a sight that never failed to enchant Jenny however often she saw it.

Other animals came too—a family of warthogs, two sable antelope; an elephant, its trumpeting and noisy splashing of water almost as loud as the sounds the lion made.

More than ever, Jenny understood what Joshua had achieved with the building of the platform. She had been convinced that it would be garish, a jarring feature in a wilderness landscape. It was not jarring at all. Since her revalation earlier in the afternoon she was not even surprised that this should be so. Joshua would make a success of Impalavlei. At last Jenny knew wholeheartedly that all he had done was for the best, even for the correct motives. He had brought water to the animals because he was concerned about them, just as he had risked his life to save the impala because he had cared about what man's carelessness had done to the small creature.

His other improvements were not for the benefit of the animals; they were for the comfort of the guests who would come to the game park. Once Jenny had condemned him because she had thought that he saw Impalavlei only as an investment. Today she understood that there was something right in his insistence that the game park should stand on its own feet. Only that way could it be accorded the respect that was its due.

It was growing darker. Beneath the platform the lion was clearly visible, but on the far bank the animals that still moved there were becoming an undistinguishable mass. In the west the sun was about to sink below the horizon, a small patch of western sky still aglow with the vivid colours of the African sunset. There would be no lingering dusk. Once the sun had vanished it would grow dark quickly. Even if the lion were to leave the scene—an eventuality which at the moment did not seem likely—driving would be dangerous; there was always the risk that an animal crossing the road might be run over.

Joshua had been very quiet. It was as if he were preoccupied with thoughts of his own. Now he spoke into the stillness. 'We'll be spending the night here, Jenny.'

She turned to him. It was just light enough to make out the clean chiselled lines of his face, the sensual lips, the high forehead, the firm jaw. There was strength in the face, coupled with a hint of latent ruthlessness. There was also integrity. She wondered how she could ever have missed it.

'I know,' she said in a small voice. 'Think we'll be all right?'

'Sure to.' His tone was reassuring. 'I'd like to make a fire, but with all the dry wood it wouldn't be wise. It will be a long cold night, Jenny. We'll have to keep each other warm.'

As an arm went around her shoulders and drew her to him, she stiffened. She had wanted this contact so badly that it was only by making her limbs rigid that she could prevent herself from turning and melting into his arms.

'Relax, poppet. I said nothing about raping you. But if we don't keep warm we could die of exposure.'

That was all their closeness meant to him. Survival through bodily contact. Oh, there had been times when he had made his enjoyment of her very clear. But even then his emotions had never been involved, and having seen Maybelle, Jenny understood why. The woman had a sultry beauty that she herself could not hope to compete with.

'Jenny!'

It was an order, and after a moment she did relax. As his arm tightened around her she made herself soft and pliant. Joshua, the man who was accustomed to being obeyed, would think she had understood the sense of his words; that she knew they would both suffer apart. He would never know that there was bliss in moulding herself to the contours of his body, in smelling the warm male smell that seemed to cling to him always, in feeling the rhythmic beat of his heart and the hard lines of his chest and arms.

It would be a long night, Joshua had said. As she let her cheek lie against the bareness of skin just beneath the base of his neck, Jenny thought the night could not be long enough. No matter that the air grew very cold with the setting of the sun, nor that neither she nor Joshua had thought to bring warm clothes. To Jenny it was as if this night was the last reality, the last happiness. When she left Impalavlei her life would be only half lived.

With the realisation came the memory of the letter. She had been about to tell Joshua of her decision when he had made the brave dash to rescue the impala, and she had not given it thought again.

Now was the time to talk to him. Linda, the applicant, would be arriving within the next few days for the interview. She would be ready to start work immediately, she had said in her letter. That being the case, once she had been trained—and that would not take long—there was nothing to keep Jenny at Impalavlei.

She opened her mouth. But strangely the words that should have been so easy did not come. For at that moment weakness took her whole body, paralysing her mind with it, so that she could not speak.

'Comfortable?' he asked, his lips still against her hair.

'Yes. And you?'

'Immensely so.' She heard him laugh, that soft seductive laugh that did such alarming things to her pulse rate. 'I could hardly be otherwise when I have a desirable woman in my arms.'

It was so long since he had spoken this way. Not since Maybelle's visit had there been anything remotely sensual between them. Even while a small sane voice told her that Joshua was an expert at knowing what women liked to hear, she thrilled to the words.

'You find me desirable?' The question seemed to emerge of its own volition.

'You're inviting me to show you?'

In the past she had tried, initially at least, to resist him. Not this time. The hunger inside her was a painful gnawing thing. She had been too long denied the rapture of his lovemaking. She knew too that the memory of it would have to last a long time. Forever probably.

She was pliant as he drew her down against his lap so that her back rested on his thigh. As his head came down towards hers she reached for his shoulders, clinging to them, as if in some way she could hold on to him. As his mouth began a sensual path upwards from her throat to her mouth, hovering tantalisingly around the corners of her lips, then to her eyes and her ears, lingering there to nibble at one lobe before travelling to the other, Jenny was swept by a sensual ache that was becoming familiar.

'God, Jenny, I've wanted you!' Joshua groaned.

And then he was kissing her again. Now the lightness was gone, and his mouth was demanding, possessive, staking a claim to which he had no right, yet one which Jenny yearned to give. Her fingers found the hair at the back of his head, knotting themselves in it, clutching at it. He did not have to force her lips open, they parted willingly, thirstily.

His thighs were hard aginst her back, and there was an extra tightening hardness which told her that he wanted her just as much as she wanted him.

With his lips still on hers his hands went to her blouse, opening it deftly and slipping it from her shoulders. And then hands and mouth were shaping themselves to the contours of her shoulders and her throat, and last of all her breasts. There was no preventing the shudder of desire as his lips closed on a nipple, no preventing the hardening of her breasts. There was just the ache of fulfilment, the knowledge that no matter if she never saw him again, if he was shortly to be another woman's husband, this night belonged to them alone: nobody else featured.

Joshua lifted away and looked down at her. It was too dark now to see his expression, but she heard his ragged breathing, felt the thudding heartbeat that was as rapid as her own.

'I want you, Jenny.'

The huskiness caught at her emotions. From this big self-sufficient man it was particularly moving. And oh, God, she wanted him too. She had never wanted anything so much in her life.

'Yes . . .'

'Jenny! Darling, I don't want to stop, not now. Do you want me too?'

Darling . . . Dimly the endearment burned in her brain. Later that night she would wonder whether it had had any significance, or whether it was just a word said in the height of emotion. But this moment was not for thinking.

'Yes,' she whispered. 'Yes, Joshua, I want you.'

He undressed her quickly yet with a surprising gentleness. Through his movements she felt the contained impatience of passion. Yet throughout his concern was for her. She huddled on the wooden floor as he undressed himself. It was quite cold now, yet her own coldness was more the momentary bereftness of separation.

And then he was holding her again, laying her gently down on the floor, shaping himself against curves and hollows that seemed made for him.

There was a sudden roar. For some time now the lion had been quiet. Now roar upon roar split the darkness. The first roar set Jenny quivering. And then as Joshua gathered her closer, caressing her soft bare limbs, warming her with his body, the shock subsided. Joshua began to kiss her again, and it seemed to Jenny as if the lion's fury and the darkness of the night and the unusual bed upon which she lay, all together heightened the drama of a very special moment.

Joshua's lovemaking became more urgent. His kisses had a new passion, his exploring hands a greater sensuousness. The lion was forgotten, its raging drowned out by the thundering in her own ears as Jenny responded to Joshua with a passion of her own.

When she thought she could bear the hunger no longer, he took her. Afterwards they lay quietly, still close together, with Joshua's arms around the slender body, keeping it warm.

'Any regrets?' he asked after what seemed a long while.

'None.' She smiled up at him, even though she knew he could not see her face. She thought perhaps the smile came through to her voice.

'I'm glad,' he said quietly. 'Let's get dressed, Jenny, then we'll sleep.'

It took Jenny longer than usual to pull on shirts and jeans, for her limbs were heavy and languid with the aftermath of their lovemaking. In the dark she saw Joshua reaching out for her. As she lay down beside him his arms closed around her.

There was no passion now. Yet as she lay against him, every inch of her body in contact with his for the warmth they could give each other, she felt the sweetness of fulfilment in her system. Earlier she had sensed that she would not forget this day. Now, with his legs curled around the shape of her body, with his chest hard at her back, with his breath, warm and clean, fanning her neck, she knew that every detail of the last hours would be forever engraved on her memory.

A stranger seeing them now might take them for husband and wife. For just this night, if it was what she wanted, she could pretend it was so. Joshua's breathing had steadied, it had become long and slow. He was asleep, Jenny knew, and thought there was something appealingly vulnerable in the idea of a man so strong and vital succumbing to sleep. For herself, she did not care if she lay awake all night. Never again would she lie in Joshua's arms. It seemed a shame to waste a minute of the night in oblivion.

She must have slept after all. For a few moments when she awoke she did not know where she was. There was an unfamiliar cold feeling and the mattress seemed hard. There was also a strange sensation of loneliness, as if something was missing.

And then the blur of sleep receded and her eyes focused on a pair of long strong legs, so near to her that she could see the dark hairs that curled on the calves. Of their own volition her eyes travelled upward.

'Sleep well, Jenny?'

Joshua was laughing down at her. His face had a fresh look despite the growth of hair on his cheeks and his chin. His eyes were sparkling and alert and his teeth were wickedly white against his tan.

'Just fine,' she smiled back at him. 'Where's breakfast, Joshua? I'm starving!'

'You don't frighten me with that.' He squatted down beside her and offered her the bottle he carried at his belt. 'There's just a bit of water left. No cup, I'm afraid.'

There was no squeamishness as she drank from the opening where his lips must have been. She loved Joshua, and loving was sharing, and this might be the last sharing they would experience.

When she gave him back the bottle he handed her a piece of biltong. 'Forgot I had it last night,' he said, as she bit with relish on the stick of dried meat.

Her eyes went sideways to the impala. It was standing, experimentally moving the injured leg. 'Be fine in a day or two,' Joshua commented.

Strange how memory returned bit by bit. For the first conscious moments there had only been the thought of their lovemaking. Now all of yesterday's events came rushing back.

'The lion?' she asked breathlessly.

'Must have wandered off while we were sleeping. There's no sign of it.'

'It could be hiding in the bush . . .' Jenny bit her lip as she looked at the stretch of ground between the foot of the ladder and the Land Rover.

'I don't think so.'

Joshua pointed to the prints on the sandy ground. Pug prints in crazy circles, where the lion had done its thwarted pacing, and then, leading away towards the distant high grass, one set of prints. It was safe to go.

Looking down at her jeans, Jenny was aware for the first time of her dishevelled appearance. Her blouse was crumpled, her jeans too. Touching a hand to her hair, she realised that it was even wilder than usual. She ran her fingers through it, then gave up the effort when she understood that only a thorough brushing would help.

'I must look an absolute sight,' she said ruefully.

'The eternal female!' His laughter rang out, low and amused, setting the blood racing in her veins as it always did. 'You do look a sight, Jenny. George will probably be sending out a search party if we don't get back soon, otherwise I'd show you just how much the sight turns me on.'

Her cheeks grew warm under a gaze that took in the very feminine figure under the crumpled clothes. It was a gaze that held the knowing look of one who knew exactly what the clothes concealed. A thudding heart told Jenny that she would not have resisted Joshua had he decided to make love to her again, George's anxiety notwithstanding.

What had happened to the girl who had repulsed her fiancé's lovemaking because they were not yet married? That Jenny Malloy had had principles which were iron-cast, which she had not thought to doubt or to bend. That same girl had been transformed into a woman who was passionate and responsive, who loved a man so deeply that she felt she would be only half living when she had returned to Pretoria.

The letter . . . She must tell Joshua about the letter this morning, before they got back to camp. After what had happened between them last night she could keep it from him no longer.

'George *will* be worried,' she said in a small voice. 'Let's go, Joshua.'

Joshua went down the ladder, the impala in his arms, and Jenny followed him. The air was crisp and chilly; the trees and bushes at the edge of the clearing were heavy with dew. On the river bank a few kudu were treading the sand on their way to the water.

'Think the platform will be a success?' Joshua asked, when he had loaded the impala into the Land Rover and was negotiating the vehicle towards the road.

'Very much so.'

'I told you once that we'd make a go of things together. We've come a long way, Jenny.'

It was hard to meet the smiling eyes, particularly when her own were filled with unshed tears. Her throat was so full that it was hard to speak, yet she had no option. The opportunity had presented itself, and she had to take it.

'Yes . . . But you'll be on your own from now on,' she told him in a choked voice, and knew that emotion had forced out words very different from the ones she had rehearsed.

The car lurched for just a split moment, then Joshua had it under control once more. Through her distress Jenny did not observe that the hands that gripped the wheel were white-knuckled.

'Perhaps you'd better explain,' he said in a dry voice.

'I . . . I'm going back to Pretoria.' It was more difficult than ever to talk through a throat that was suddenly parched. Difficult too to address herself to a stony-faced man who had all at once become a stranger.

'To your career?'

'Yes.' And then, to add strength to what might appear a flimsy excuse, 'And to Bruce.'

He shot her a keen look. His eyes were narrowed and mocking, his lips tight. Then he asked, 'You're getting married?'

'Er . . . yes, I am.' She shifted her eyes, knowing the hesitation had lasted a moment too long.

If he reminded her of the evening in Pretoria, when Bruce had been anything but a pining fiancé, she would not be able to come up with an appropriate answer. Not now, not when it required all her control to keep her voice from breaking and the tears from spilling.

But it seemed Joshua was not concerned with Bruce. He asked, in a level tone that was entirely free from expression, 'What do you intend doing about Impalavlei?'

'I haven't made up my mind yet.' She looked at him, the elfin face pleading for understanding. 'As far as my duties are concerned, I won't let you down, Joshua.'

There was no softening in the lines of the grimly-set mouth. 'Sounds as if you're planning to do just that.'

'No.' Her voice was low and unhappy. 'I . . . I have everything in hand. I advertised . . . for a Girl Friday. And . . .' she stopped to swallow hard, 'a girl is coming out for an interview.' Another pleading glance at the stony-faced man at her side. 'She . . . she sounds just right. Her name is Linda Ainsley.'

The Land Rover took the tarred road smoothly and easily. The white-knuckled hands had relaxed their grip. The ascetic profile was fixed on the road. Just as if she had not said anything of importance, Jenny thought with a touch of despair.

'Don't you have any comments?' she asked at length.

Grey eyes turned and subjected her to a chill scrutiny. 'You're not going back to Bruce any more than you'll give up Impalavlei.'

'I don't know why you say that,' she managed bumpily.

'I do.' His tone was terse. 'I don't believe you'd go back to a spineless milksop with whom you've no chance of happiness.'

She raised her chin in what she hoped was a gesture of defiance. 'You don't know that.'

'Like hell I don't!'

The car lurched to a halt and the next moment Jenny found herself seized by the shoulders and pulled roughly across the seat. Joshua gave her no time to protest as his mouth covered hers in a kiss that was possessive and erotically sensual. Through her outrage Jenny found her senses responding; as he pulled her even closer, she shuddered and arched closer against him.

The kiss ended as abruptly as it had begun, and when Joshua released her Jenny stared at him bewildered.

'That's to show you just how much I do know,' he ground out violently, in answer to her unspoken question. 'Don't tell me that idiot Bruce arouses you, because I wouldn't believe it. If he did, you'd have been with him all along.' A pause. A gleam appeared in his eyes. 'You *are* aroused by me.'

She did not deny it. Things had gone so far between them that a denial would have been absurd. If there was something to say, she did not know what it was.

Neither could she explain to herself his outraged reaction to her announcement that she was returning to Bruce. His insistence on proving to her, in his own inimitable way, that her feelings for Bruce were not to be compared with her feelings for Joshua himself. Hope flickered suddenly inside her like a small wild bird—a crazy hope, totally without reason.

Hope that was crushed by his next words. 'About a Girl Friday. I approve.'

'You . . . you do?'

'Absolutely. A hand reached for her chin, cupping it, defying her to look away. 'Linda, you said her name is? When is she coming?'

'In . . . in the next few days.' Her voice was so low that she barely heard it herself.

'Excellent. I hope she'll prove suitable.'

He was glad she was going! How foolish she had been to think otherwise, even for a minute.

With a jerk she freed her chin. 'I hope so too.' Her voice was as firm as she could make it—no easy feat when her throat was choked with tears. 'I'll be leaving Impalavlei as soon as Linda is trained.'

'No, my darling,' he said very softly, 'you're going nowhere.'

Jenny stared at him with eyes that were wide and moist and luminous. 'What . . . what did you say?'

'That you're not leaving here. At least not without me.' Unexpectedly his voice was ragged.

She was trying to make sense of the words when he drew her to him and held her close. She could feel his lips in her hair as they had been last night. She let her own lips find the patch of bare skin between buttons.

'You will marry me, Jenny darling?'

She lifted her head, tilting it backward to look at him through a haze of joy. 'Oh yes, Joshua, yes!' And then, 'But Maybelle . . .?'

'Nothing more than a friend. She was impressed with Impalavlei. She'll be bringing tours this way.'

To Maybelle Joshua was more than a friend. Jenny remembered the adoring looks she had given him, the possessiveness of her manner, but wisely she said nothing. Maybelle's beauty was such that she would attract other men.

There was one more thing she had to know. 'The Girl Friday idea appeals to you. Darling, why?'

His fingers went to her hair, winding through it, letting his hand rest on her throat, sending her too responsive pulses racing. 'Because your Linda will free you from your duties. Impalavlei will always be home, Jenny darling. But we won't be here all the year round. We'll be making trips to America—I have interests there too. I'd like to think we'd be leaving our game park in good hands.'

He looked down into eyes that were radiant. 'Will you mind the hectic pace, my darling Jenny?'

She was about to reply, when his lips came down on hers. She would have told him that just being with him was her total happiness. Whether at Impalavlei or elsewhere. But Joshua's kiss grew harder, more passionate. As her own lips parted in response she knew that no words were necessary. Now and always Joshua would know what she felt.